“The Solon and Beyond.

Kryptos, CIA headquarters, Langley, Virginia, USA

Unauthorized Dan Brown Update

W. Frederick Zimmerman, NIMBLE BOOKS LLC

DISCLAIMER: This book is unofficial and unauthorized. It is not authorized, approved, licensed, or endorsed by Dan Brown, his publishers, or licensors. Any use of the trademarks and character names is strictly for the purpose of analysis and news reporting. All material related to the Dan Brown publications is (c) Dan Brown and (c) Doubleday Publishing. All material related to "The Da Vinci Code" film is (c) Columbia Pictures.

NIMBLE BOOKS

ISBN: 0-9754479-9-8

Library of Congress Pre-assigned Control Number (PCN): N/A

This document last saved 2006-05-15.

Wherever possible, quoted news articles, internet postings, and other works are attributed by author, title, date, and web location. Every effort has been made to secure permission to use works quoted in this book, and if an oversight is drawn to our attention, Nimble Books will gladly include an acknowledgement.

The cover page illustration is *Kryptos,* on the grounds of the Central Intelligence Agency, Langley, Virginia, USA.

Table of Contents

Book description

Through the magic of print-on-demand technology, **this "nimble" guide to the works of best-selling author Dan Brown provides the latest news about the author and his works,** *updated whenever there are significant developments.* Unlike a conventional book, for which editions are printed in quantity every couple of years, this "living book" goes through frequent "mini-editions" and is printed fresh whenever customers place an order. This version was most recently updated on May 15, 2006 with the addition of more than 60 new pages, including Dan Brown's full witness statement in his London plagiarism trial.

The *Unauthorized Dan Brown Update* includes information about *Digital Fortress, Angels & Demons, Deception Point, The Da Vinci Code* (book and movie), and *The Solomon Key*. It's a "meta" book in the sense that it complements, without trying to replace, the many worthy books that are already available about *The Da Vinci Code.* This *Update* is unique in that it provides a "nimble," timely report on Dan Brown's entire *oeuvre,* including everything that is known about *The Solomon Key,* "The Da Vinci Code" movie, and beyond. The *Update* gathers, analyzes, and synthesizes the best information that is publicly available about Dan Brown and his work.

Read this book if ...

- You like to stay up to date on favorite authors such as Dan Brown.
- You enjoyed Dan Brown's books, including *The Da Vinci Code.*
- You want a guide to the best books and websites about Dan Brown and his works.
- You want to know about *The Solomon Key.*
- You want to know about the Tom Hanks/Ron Howard movie version of *The Da Vinci Code.*

Don't bother if …

- You think Dan Brown is a hack.
- You want to read a 500-page treatise about early Gnostic history.
- You want to read a detailed 500-page refutation of everything that is incorrect about *The Da Vinci Code.*
- You are a highly literal-minded fundamentalist Christian.
- You are a highly *un*-literal-minded New Age mystic.

This *Update* is for book fans who think Dan Brown can tell a good story, not for zealots (of any persuasion) who never read fiction.

What this mini-book contains

- What to know (my two cents) if you missed *Digital Fortress, Angels & Demons,* or *Deception Point.*
- Pointers to good books and articles about Dan Brown's previous works, including *The Da Vinci Code.*
- The latest news about movies based on Dan Brown's books.
- Careful summary, attribution, and evaluation of all the published news about *The Solomon Key.*

What this mini-book does *not* contain

- Detailed factual, artistic, historic, theological, religious, and symbological analysis of *The Da Vinci Code* or any of Brown's other previous works.

Publisher's comments

This *Update* will be available in e-book and paperback editions from fine retailers like Amazon.com.

How to decide between paperback and PDF/LIT

If you are struggling to decide whether to buy the paperback version of this book or the e-book versions (Adobe's PDF and Microsoft's Reader or LIT format), here's a simple table comparing the benefits.

Paperback	**PDF**
Color cover, b&w interior	Color throughout with hyperlinks
Hold, dog-ear, throw.	Search, save, print.

In other words, it's a matter of personal preference. The content is exactly the same in both versions. And either way, you get a free PDF update.

How to subscribe to updates of this book

Purchase of this book entitles you to a free PDF update anytime in the next 12 months.

If you send a **proof of purchase** (typically, an e-mail receipt from Amazon.com or other fine retailers) for *either* the paperback or electronic versions of the book **via e-mail to danbrown-updates@nimblebooks.com,** we will send you a free update via PDF.

Tip: Don't bother asking your retailer for a free update! They won't know what you are talking about and aren't set up to help you. You must contact Nimble Books directly via danbrown-updates@nimblebooks.com.

Unfortunately, we can't offer the free update in paperback form, since it costs us money to print and ship each copy.

For those who are curious about how often we update, the answer is that it is determined by the intersection of the occurrence of significant news and the sensible management of costs. It is not free to update the source file for a book–it costs at least a week's worth of revenue. So we try to be strategic about when we do updates–but we love taking advantage of technology to deliver a superior product!

Author's comments

I decided to write this book when I finally read and enjoyed *The Da Vinci Code* in late 2004. I had studiously avoided the massive bestseller because I had read and been unimpressed by Brown's first book, *Digital Fortress.* Frankly, I thought *DF* was pretty dumb and clanky ... but *Da Vinci* was clearly a much better book, with high idea density and dozens of intricately plotted puzzles. I was amazed by the improvement between his first book and his fourth. He's a young guy, and it looks like it will be worthwhile to track his work for a long time to come.

I learned a lot of fascinating things in the course of my research. Here are some of the discoveries you will share when you accompany me on this journey.

- Brown had a significant career as a singer/songwriter.
- He wrote a "self-help" book for women before he ever became a novelist.
- He wrote a great on-line list of 7 tips to selling a novel–and it is available free on-line.
- He has outlines for twelve (12) future Robert Langdon novels.
- *The Solomon Key* may be tied to an ancient Masonic phrase, "Is there no hope for the widow's son?"
- His literary career at this point (book #5) is running ahead of the authors he considers his role models.
- Why Ron Howard cast Tom Hanks as Robert Langdon.

Author bio

W. Frederick Zimmerman is the publisher of Nimble Books LLC. He lives in Ann Arbor, Michigan, with his wife, Cheryl, and their children Kelsey and Parker.

Acknowledgements

My beautiful wife Cheryl, who urged to read something by Dan Brown for years.

About Nimble Books

Our trusty Merriam-Webster Collegiate Dictionary defines "nimble" as follows:

> 1: quick and light in motion: AGILE *nimble fingers*
>
> 2 a: marked by quick, alert, clever conception, comprehension, or resourcefulness *a nimble mind* b: RESPONSIVE, SENSITIVE *a nimble listener*

And traces the etymology to the 14th Century:

> Middle English nimel, from Old English numol holding much, from niman to take; akin to Old High German neman to take, Greek nemein to distribute, manage, nomos pasture, nomos usage, custom, law

The etymology is reminiscent of the old Biblical adage, "to whom much is given, much is expected" (Luke 12:48). Nimble Books seeks to honor that Christian principle by combining the spirit of *nimbleness* with the Biblical concept of *abundance:* we deliver what you need to know about a subject in a quick, resourceful, and sensitive manner.

Editorial reviews

Author & source:

Greg Taylor, TheDailyGrail.com, February 16, 2005[1]

Review:

> For hard-core Dan Brown fans, there is a new e-Book available from Amazon.com titled Unauthorized Dan Brown Update for $7.95, which gives the low-down on the past, present and future of this almost unknown author (*cough*). This short book (69 pages), published by Nimble Books, is a basic introduction and resource for those wanting to know more about the man and his books

[1] http://www.dailygrail.com/node/964

(and forthcoming movie[s]). Unauthorized Dan Brown Update is not an involved look at the topics Brown writes about, but is more a resource document for the serious Dan fans out there. Thanks Fred.

Here's what I posted in response:

Thanks, Greg. You hit the nail on the head -- this "living book" is intended to be a launch pad for Dan Brown fans. It will get longer as Dan's ouevre expands!

I thought it would be redundant to provide elaborate treatment of the books already published, so I plan to take advantage of the book's electronic publishing format to provide "lightning" updates as news about THE SOLOMON KEY (and subsequent works) becomes available. People who buy the UPDATE are entitled to a free PDF update at any time in the first year after publication.

The other thing that differentiates the book from most of the "Da Vinci" books I've seen is perspective ... the UPDATE is written less for the person who likes gnostics and more for the person who likes gnovelists. ;-)

May I say, BTW, that your book on THE SOLOMON KEY is excellent.

Cheers,

Fred

Editorial reviews of other works by Nimble Books

Author & source:

Greg S. Davidson, Amazon.com review.[2]

Review

I loved the information in the "Unofficial 'Half-Blood Prince' Update", because I am a Harry Potter fan, and me and my kids will be in that bookstore at 12:01 am on whatever day the next volumes emerge, but I was even more interested in the methodology used to sift and assess all those random bits of information (lost sheep?) roaming the internet. This is a pathfinder for a fundamentally new kind of book, and I would be

[2] http://tinyurl.com/4rx6 x

interested in seeing the same methodology applied elsewhere. And as an added bonus the author's prose is both lively and concise, making this a very pleasurable book to read.

Author & source:

Mimi Cummins, HPBook6.com.[3]

Review

The author of this book … is taking advantage of "Print On Demand" technology to update the book whenever new information has been released … This is an excellent example of the merits of Print On Demand technology in that it allows the author to make sure that the book never becomes outdated. Kudos to the author for not only providing a very well written book full of interesting and pertinent information, but also for using new technologies that allows his readers to keep up to date.

[3] http://www.hpbook6.com

Christianity and *The Da Vinci Code*

As a Christian I feel responsible to comment on the theology of *The Da Vinci Code.* Fortunately, my position is quite simple.

If, as I do, you accept that the Four Gospels (Matthew, Mark, Luke, and John) are the authentic, divinely inspired Word of God, then *The Da Vinci Code* is simply fiction–clever, enjoyable, provocative fiction, but fiction nonetheless. The reason is that there are too many statements in those Gospels that are completely inconsistent with the provocative ideas in *The Da Vinci Code.*

If, like many, you are not sure whether the Four Gospels are the final Word, I urge you to read *The Da Vinci Code* with a discerning mind. Start with the Bible as we have it today. If the theories Dan Brown puts forward had been found persuasive in previous centuries, his book would not be in the "fiction" section of the bookstore, and there would be a billion Gnostic Bibles in print, instead of a billion Bibles that affirm the divinity of Christ.

If you are a skeptic or an agnostic, have fun reading this work of fiction ... but ask yourself once or twice, in the small wee hours of the morning when your soul is quiet, why is this particular thriller such a best seller? Can you come up with a respectful explanation of why the story of Christ is still so important to so many people?

Dan Brown's Music

Dan Brown's career began in music. This profile in the student newspaper at his alma mater, Amherst College, provides the prehistory.

> Brown … sang in the Glee Club, played the piano … and went to Hollywood with hopes of pursuing a musical career—an endeavor which culminated in his writing a song that was performed at the 1996 Olympic Games in Atlanta …
>
> Brown specifically loved playing the piano and feels that he was able to focus in on creating an original sound while he was here. His experiences singing and touring with the Glee Club opened his eyes to new things on their World Tour trip in 1983.[4]

I went to a similar school, Swarthmore College, graduating in 1982, so I think I have a fairly good image of what it was like to be an "artsy" student at a top liberal arts college in that era. The first thing you have to remember is that Amherst is extremely selective and expensive, so Brown was surrounded by smart people who had all the tools to succeed in life. Staking out an identity as a musician is one of the riskier career moves you can make coming out of a top liberal arts college... the preponderance of students at places like Amherst and Swarthmore wind up being professionals with advanced degrees, working for the elite institutions of the world. It's not that the top liberal arts colleges don't support the arts ...they do, and they provide excellent training. But in many ways the easier path is to follow a course into the professional class. Brown showed a lot of guts by what he did after graduation.

Was Brown's music any good?

The verdict seems to be mixed. His CDs are very difficult to find, and I haven't yet been able to track down any to form my own opinion. Any reader tips sent via e-mail to danbrown@nimblebooks.com would be much appreciated!

---

[4] Mary Sarro-Waite, The Amherst Student Online, 2001-2002, issue 7; http://halogen.note.amherst.edu/~astudent/2001-2002/issue07/news/03.html

Having a song performed at the Olympics is a nice achievement, but it's not exactly winning a Grammy. The Olympic song was called "Peace in Our Time."[5] Tragically for Brown obsessives, the song did not make the official Olympic music CD, "Rhythm of the Games.".[6] Apparently Brown was aced out by the Boyz II Men rendition of the "Star Spangled Banner."

Track Listings

1. Impossible Dream - Tevin Campbell
2. Everlasting Love - Mary J. Blige
3. Reaching for My Goal - Brian McKnight
4. Imagine - Corey Glover
5. Dreamin' - Usher
6. Champion's Theme - Kenny G.
7. You Gotta Believe in Love - Soul for Real
8. Reach - Gloria Estefan
9. Wildflower - Cedric "K-Ci" Hailey
10. You're a Winner - The Tony Rich Project
11. What Am I Doing Here - Jordan Hill
12. Star Spangled Banner - Boyz II Men

Track Listing for "Rhythm of the Games" at Amazon.com.

A retrospective endorsement from producer Barry Fasman is friendly, but does not suggest that Brown made a huge mistake in becoming a novelist.

> "It was his own brand of pop, real accessible mainstream," says Los Angeles music producer Barry Fasman, who worked with Brown. [7]

---

[5] David Mehegan, Boston Globe, 5/8/2004, http://www.boston.com/news/globe/living/articles/2004/05/08/thriller_instinct/)

[6] http://www.amazon.com/exec/obidos/tg/detail/-/B000008QOW/002-0231346-9340014?v=glance

[7] David Mehegan, Boston Globe, 5/8/2004, http://www.boston.com/news/globe/living/articles/2004/05/08/thriller_instinct/)

According to one article,

> ...his brand of *middle-of-the-road pop* failed to sell. [emphasis added][8]

"Middle of the road pop" seems like a plausible characterization given Brown's taste in movies, described in in the same FAQ – "Annie Hall," "Fantasia," Zeffirelli's "Romeo and Juliet."

In a 1998 interview, Brown himself was not terribly enthusiastic.

> I lived in Hollywood CA for a while, doing the songwriting thing. Aside from a song in the Atlanta Olympic ceremonies, I never had much success in music.[9]

How to channel Brown's music tastes

It's too late for most of us to catch Dan Brown in the Amherst Glee Club, and his post-college CDs seem to have disappeared into the mists of time. So for deep fans of Dan Brown the author, perhaps the best way to "channel" Brown's musical tastes is to listen to some of the same music that Brown does.

> I've recently become hooked on the Spanish singer Franco de Vita. I also listen to The Gypsy Kings, Enya, Sarah Mclachlan, and (if I'm feeling old) the very young and talented songwriter Vanessa Carlton. [10]

In subsequent editions of this *Update,* I will add a few paragraphs commenting on the experience of reading the Brown *oeuvre* while listening to his favorite music.

---

[8] Dan Glaister, The Guardian, August 6, 2004; http://books.guardian.co.uk/departments/generalfiction/story/0,6000,1277339,00.html

[9] http://www.writerswrite.com/journal/may98/brown.htm

[10] http://www.danbrown.com/meet_dan/faq.html

187 Men to Avoid: A Survival Guide for the Romantically Frustrated Woman

Dan and his wife Blythe (also known as Danielle) wrote this slender volume together for publication in August 1995. Frankly, this looks like what my Books I Won't Be Reading blog (http://www.nimblebooks.com/wordpress/category/books-i-wont-be-reading/) pegs as a "non-book" – something so fluffy and research-free that it doesn't really deserve to be called a book.

(Not that there's anything wrong with that! One of my first experiences in publishing was writing an outline for a computer book knockoff of the early 80's hit *Real Men Don't Eat Quiche.* My masterpiece was to have been called *Real Users Don't Read the Manual.)*

The public responds to 187 Men

The first review appeared on the Internet on July 17, 1995, as Usenet poster "Linda9163" wrote:

> The new humor book "187 Men To Avoid" just became my new dating bible. I think I've met about 173 of them!!!![11]

Although the publication date was August 1995, it's normal for books to be in stores a few weeks before the nominal publication date, and there's nothing to suggest that this was "review spam" planted by Dan Brown or his publisher.

A couple of years later (and before Dan Brown's ascension to publishing's Valhalla), the book earned a more mixed review from Internet poster "rogermw".

> While strolling through the bookstore one day, I came across a little illustrated humor book for women who are

[11] Usenet Sdnet.singles, http://tinyurl.com/7ytdv [via Google Groups]

down on their luck in the dating department, entitled "187 men to avoid."

Right out of the starting gate, number 2 of the 187 men to avoid was "Men who eat Kraft Macaroni and Cheese more than once per week".

Well, that kicks ME out of the running. (There was also an entry for "Men who know the lyrics to the Gilligan's Island theme song", but fortunately no entry for men who eat Fruity Pebbles or Lucky Charms. They're magically delicious, you know.)[12]

The reviews at Amazon.com were mixed. One anonymous (and perhaps overly literal-minded) male reader commented:

[m]y sister read this book, then asked me to read it and give her a "man's opinion." … I could just as easily have drawn up a list of 187 women to avoid. But after exhaustively enumerating every unpleasant character trait, that would leave me with no women left who did not fit into at least one of the 187 categories. … The secret to a successful social life is accepting peoples bad points and loving a person for their flaws as well as their good points.

I'm not saying there certainly are men that should be avoided; drug dealers, sociopaths, abusive and manipulative men. But to go to the extreme that this book has gone to will make you very lonely for a very long time.[13]

Well, sure, but the point of a book like this is not that it's scientific or logically accurate, but whether it gives you something fun to think and talk about, as another anonymous reader pointed out.

I gave this book to my sister-in-law for her birthday and we laughed for hours. Great observations about men. Definitely a girl book![14]

From these limited data points, my evaluation is that *187 Men* was a modest success for the authors. It generated some positive buzz, got them familiar with the world of publishing, and gave them some useful experience.

---

[12] Usenet rec.arts.tv.ms3tk, http://tinyurl.com/5yyes via Google Groups

[13] http://www.amazon.com/exec/obidos/tg/detail/-/0425147835/qid=1105393032/sr=8-2/ref=sr_8_xs_ap_i2_xgl14/002-0231346-9340014?v=glance&s=books&n=507846

[14] http://www.amazon.com/exec/obidos/tg/detail/-/0425147835/qid=1105393032/sr=8-2/ref=sr_8_xs_ap_i2_xgl14/002-0231346-9340014?v=glance&s=books&n=507846

How to acquire 187 Men

This book is extremely difficult to find ... it's out of print and listed as "out of stock" on most Internet bookstores. You might try an interlibrary loan via your local public library. By way of setting expectations, Michigan's inter-library book exchange system, which seems pretty comprehensive and includes more than 100 libraries, didn't have a copy.

For what it's worth, the ISBN is **0425147835**.

If you are a book collector or a Dan Brown fanatic, keep your eyes open for this one at local garage sales.

Please don't pay the $995.29 that one Amazon.com Marketplace seller was asking in December 2004.

Digital Fortress

Digital Fortress has been out for almost seven years now, so I'm not going to beat the subject to death. I'm just going to tell you a few of the things that come most strongly to my mind when I think about Dan Brown's first novel. Nimble Books will commence much more elaborate coverage of future novels when *The Solomon Key* is published.

In a nutshell, the plot concerns the National Security Agency's response to the development of an "unbreakable" code. It's a thriller set in the world of espionage and cryptography.

Tip: If you are trying to decide whether to read *Digital Fortress,* don't start your Dan Brown experience here. It is his first book, and it shows. The following books are significantly better.

DIGITAL FORTRESS
A THRILLER
"A DISTURBING, CUTTING-EDGE TECHNO-THRILLER THAT SHOULD GALVANIZE EVERYONE WHO SENDS OR RECEIVES E-MAIL OR EVEN DREAMS OF NAVIGATING THE WEB." —JOHN L. NANCE, AUTHOR OF PANDORA'S CLOCK, BLACKOUT
DAN BROWN

Spoiler warning: everything below this line assumes that you have already read "Digital Fortress."

Smart-Ass Summary of *Digital Fortress*

NSA cryptographer Susan Whatsername and bf Generic Prof race to deal with unbreakable code built by Japanese Guy; meanwhile, Dirty Old Boss blows up NSA supercomputer to impress Susan.

No Lamborghinis in the parking lot

One of the key characters in *Digital Fortress* is an NSA cryptographer who drives a Lamborghini. I have a hard time believing that anyone at NSA drives Lamborghinis. From everything I have read, in real life NSA is a great big government bureaucracy that is structured along military lines. You don't see many Lamborghinis in the parking lot in those places.

These photographs are from the NSA's web site (so, in other words, they had plenty of time to move the Lamborghinis to the back parking lot).

National Security Agency headquarters, Fort Meade, Maryland.

No Lamborghinis visible on zoom.

The secret answer is ... 3

The solution to the puzzle at the heart of the book is ... 3. Yes, the friendly whole number that follows 2 and precedes four. Not its exotic cousin, π, or 3. 1415926535, and not its massive cousin, 3 gazillion, but plain old 3, period. No decimal points, no nothing.

I knew that the answer was three as soon as the puzzle appeared in the book. The characters took about twenty pages to figure it out.

The bad guy who poses the puzzle is supposedly a computer security expert. But he does the good guys a huge favor by having the computer tell them that "numeric input" is required. Why would any computer security expert ever do that? It makes cracking the code much, much easier.

Let's say there are a maximum of 10 digits in the password. If numeric digits are required, the maximum number of combinations is $10^{10,}$ or ten to the tenth power. That is a much, much smaller number than 36^{10}, the number of combinations that is possible if you allow A-Z and 0-9. If you allow the special characters such as @ and # (at and hash), you can get the number of combinations up to 48^{10}. As William Goldman's genius character Vizzini likes to say in his classic novel *The Princess Bride*, it is "inconceivable" that a cryptographer would deliberately weaken his security by using such an insecure procedure.

The only reason the "numeric input" is required is so that later on, when the hero and heroine "crack" the puzzle and figure out that the answer is "three" (3), there will be no ambiguity about whether to enter the word or the numeral.

Sales record for Digital Fortress

In 2004, the paperback was still selling strongly, with sales ranks near the top for most of the spring and summer, dropping off in fall, followed by a sharp rise just before Christmas.

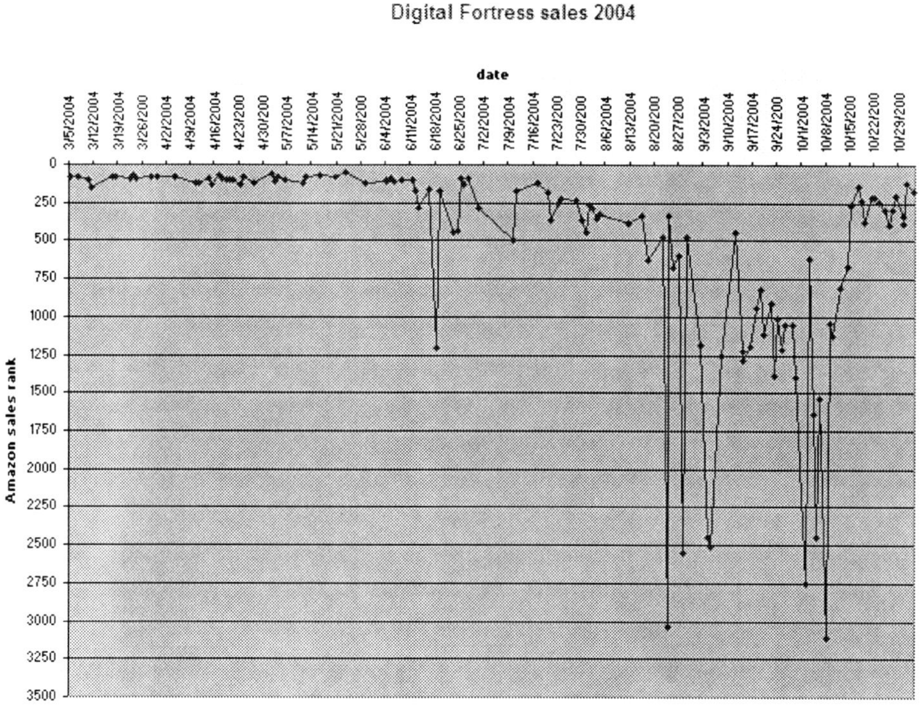
Digital Fortress sales 2004
date
3/5/2004
3/12/2004
3/19/2004
3/26/200
4/2/2004
4/9/2004
4/16/2004
4/23/200
4/30/200
5/7/2004
5/14/2004
5/21/2004
5/28/200
6/4/2004
6/11/2004
6/18/2004
6/25/200
7/2/2004
7/9/2004
7/16/2004
7/23/200
7/30/200
8/6/2004
8/13/2004
8/20/200
8/27/200
9/3/2004
9/10/2004
9/17/2004
9/24/200
10/1/2004
10/8/2004
10/15/200
10/22/200
10/29/200
Amazon sales rank
0
250
500
750
1000
1250
1500
1750
2000
2250
2500
2750
3000
3250
3500

Amazon sales ranks for the mass-market paperback of *Digital Fortress.*

According to the Internet Movie Database (IMDB), no movie plans are in the works as yet.

Angels & Demons

Again, I'm just going to tell you a few of the things that come most sharply to my mind when I think about Dan Brown's second novel.

Spoiler-free summary: Harvard symbologist Robert Langdon is asked to investigate a mystery involving science, religion, CERN, and the Vatican.

The first thing that struck me about this book is that it's shelved in the wrong section – strictly speaking, it should be in science fiction. The tip-off is delivered very early, with a reference in chapter 1 of the paperback edition to the High-Speed Civil Transport, the "prototype of the Boeing X-33." In other words, Brown explicitly states that an important plot device is a piece of technology that won't be in civilian passenger use for another five or ten years from publication date (2000). Thus, despite the "spiritually oriented" title, the world that Brown is writing about is a science fictional one set not in the present day, but in the future. And since The Da Vinci Code is a sequel to *Angels & Demons*, the same must be true for *Da Vinci*!

To my mind, this takes a lot of the pressure off reading these books. Since *Angels & Demons* and *The Da Vinci Code* are science fiction, it's not necessary to have a lot of heartburn about whether they're literally true. Obviously, they're not. They're set in an alternate future world that is a lot like ours, but has some significantly different elements. Just as the technology is more advanced than what is actually available In Real Life, so also the secret organizations in Brown's science fictional world are better organized, more cunning, and more effective than IRL. In essence, the Robert Langdon novels are an H.G. Wells-like thought experiment in imagining what the world would be like if symbologists were in charge.

Spoiler warning: everything below this line assumes that you have already read *Angels & Demons* in its entirety.

BESTSELLING AUTHOR OF DIGITAL FORTRESS
DAN BROWN
ANGELS & DEMONS
"A breathless, real-time adventure...Exciting, fast-paced, with an unusually high IQ." —San Francisco Chronicle

Smart-ass Summaries of Angels & Demons

- Pope v. Science. Science 1, Pope 0.
- The Illuminati are baaaaack! And badder than ever.
- Harvard symbologist Robert Langdon scores a free trip to Rome–and gets a girlfriend!

Things I liked about Angels & Demons

Robert Langdon is a more fully developed character in this, his first appearance, than in *The Da Vinci Code.* That actually makes sense, as Brown may have felt the need to spend a bit more time establishing the character than he did in *Da Vinci.* The biggest surprise was the episode that gives Langdon his claustrophobia. If I remember correctly, in *Da Vinci* the episode is summarized as "Langdon got stuck in a cave once." In *Angels & Demons,* the story is told in full, and I found it actually quite chilling, because it's a lot more than a kid–gets–stuck–in–a–closet story. The young Robert Langdon fell into a sinkhole and had to tread water for hours before anyone noticed him. *That* tells me something about the character ... not just that he has reason to be afraid of closed spaces, but that even as a young boy he had courage and endurance that go beyond the normal.

The Camerlengo is an amazing character–brilliantly conceived and patiently revealed.

The evolution of the global drama of faith involving the Vatican and the Illuminati is quite touching.

Things I didn't like about Angels & Demons

The comic-book treatment of CERN rang false to me, as did the mock Euro-nationalism of its director. It reminded me of, well, a simple-minded American view of the world.

Recommended Reading

If you like *Angels & Demons* a lot, Secrets of Angels & Demons: The Unauthorized Guide To The Bestselling Novel by Dan Burstein and Arne de Keijzer is a must-buy. Burstein and de Keijzer bring the same highly professional approach to this book that they do to *Secrets of the Code* (described in a later chapter).

For those with an eye for business, it's interesting that this book's Amazon sales rank seems to hover around 18,000, whereas *Secrets of the Code* is usually in the top 1,000. It's a good rule of thumb that double the sales rank means half the sales, so it's clear that the market for content about *Angels & Demons* is at least a factor of 10 less than the market for content about *The Da Vinci Code.* That's unfortunate, because there's absolutely no way that *Angels & Demons* is 10 times worse than *The Da Vinci Code,* or that its subject matter is 10 times less important. *Angels & Demons* is about faith and science; *The Da Vinci Code* is about Jesus in the modern era. The subjects ought to be pretty much on a par in terms of reader interest. That they're not is a reflection either on the primacy of Jesus or on modern readers' lack of scientific literacy; take your pick.

The Angels & Demons *movie*

According to the IMDB, no film plans are in the works as yet. The $64K question is whether Tom Hanks could possibly be persuaded to do a prequel to the movie of *The Da Vinci Code.* I'm inclined to doubt it. Why? Well, do you remember seeing "Big 0.5"? "Apollo 12"? "Philadelphia Reloaded?"

The strongest argument to the contrary is spelled $$$$$. If "The Da Vinci Code" is a hugely successful movie (which is certainly a possibility), there will be enormous financial pressure on the key players to reprise their roles. The alternative is to go forward with a similar production team, but recast Robert Langdon with a Tom Hanks lite. Roger Moore may still be available.

Dream casts for *Angels & Demons*

Here are some of the ideas that IMDB fans had about casting *Angels & Demons,* before it was announced that Hanks would play Robert Langdon in "The Da Vinci Code."

Character	**Dream Cast Ideas**	**Fred's Comments**
Robert Langdon	Russell Crowe, David Duchovny, Gerard Butler, Harrison Ford, Robert Redford ….	Isn't Harrison Ford, like, really, really old? Almost as old as Redford?
Vittoria Vetra	Angelina Jolie, Asia Argento, Monica Bellucci	Character is a brilliant and sexy marine biologist. I'm thinking Jacqueline Bisset reprising her role in "The Deep."
Commander Olivetti	Ben Kingsley	Thankless role is too lame for Kingsley. Character spends most of the novel in denial, and doesn't really get a big "redemption" or "reveal" scene. Might as well have a TV sheriff in the role.
The Hassasin	Oded Fehr	Fairly typical bad guy could be played by any up-and-coming character actor.
Carmelognelo	Jude Law	Not *another* Jude Law movie!

Deception Point

Again, I'm just going to tell you a few of the things that come most sharply to my mind when I think about Dan Brown's third novel.

Rachel Sexton, the protagonist of the novel, works for the top-secret (and quite real) National Reconnaissance Office, the organization that manages our nation's spy satellites. (http://www.nro.gov) Her estranged father is President of the United States. Much political and scientific complexity ensues as she is asked to examine the announcement that NASA has discovered life on Mars.

Visitor Center at NRO headquarters, Chantilly, Virginia

Spoiler warning: everything below this line assumes that you have already read *Deception Point.*

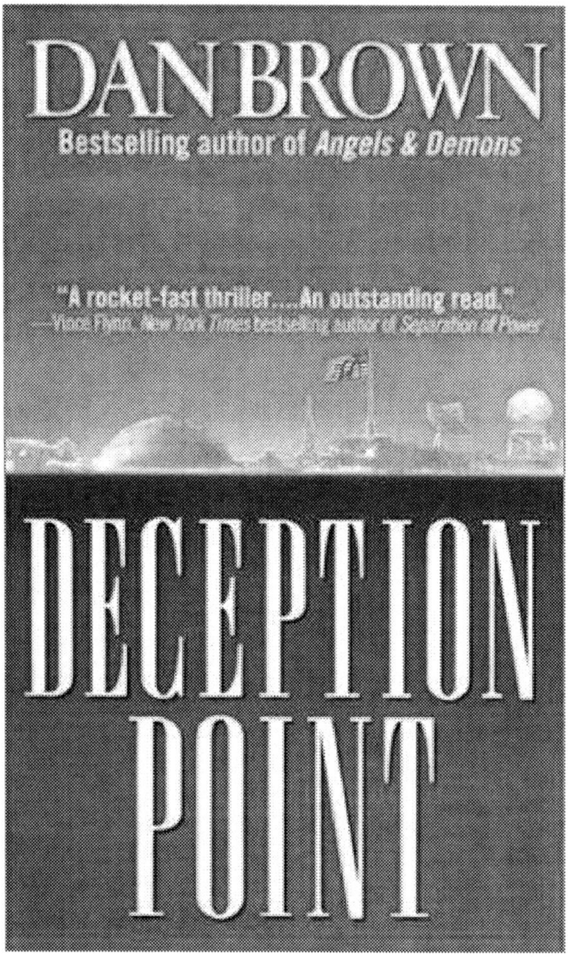
DAN BROWN
Bestselling author of Angels & Demons
"A rocket-fast thriller....An outstanding read."
DECEPTION
POINT

Smart-Ass Summary of Deception Point

NRO "gister" Rachel Sexton (who also happens to be the President's estranged daughter) figures out that a purported Mars life rock is ... something else entirely. Meanwhile, a sinister figure who MUST be played by Ron Rifkin (Sloane on "Alias") spins a massive conspiracy ... to save the NASA budget! If only real-life conspiracies were so benign ...

The Deception Point *movie*

According to the IMDB, no film plans are in the works as yet. Even so, IMDB fans already have some ideas about casting.

Character	**Dream Cast**	**Fred's Comments**
Sedgewick Sexton	Gene Hackman	According to the "New York Times" (11/15/04), Hackman's name on a DVD is an automatic sales guarantee.
Gabrielle Ashe	Gabrielle Union	Who?
Rachel Sexton	Sandra Bullock, Jill Hennessy ...	Sandra Bullock somehow seems pretty plausible for this role ... her awkwardness brings a logical justification for her estrangement from a father the President who is (among other things) a professional smoothie.
Michael Tolland	Dennis Quaid	Too old for a male lead? Not in Hollywood.
William Pickering	Robert Duvall	I see him as Ron Rifkin, the guy who plays Sloane on "Alias"

Recommended reading

Shades of Gray: National Security and the Evolution of Space Reconnaissance by L. Parker Temple, American Institute of Aeronautics and Astronautics: 2004. A recent scholarly study putting NRO in the context of American space history.

Reshaping National Intelligence for an Age of Information (RAND Studies in Policy Analysis) by Gregory F. Treverton, Jr.. RAND: 2001. The Defense Department's favorite think tank puts NRO in the context of the total system of U.S. strategic intelligence.

The Wizards of Langley: Inside the CIA's Directorate of science and Technology. By Jeffrey Richelson. Westview: 2001. No direct connection to Deception Point, but good inside dirt about satellite reconnaissance ... for example, this book broke the story of the MISTY stealth satellite.

Report of the National Commission for the Review of the National Reconnaissance Office and the Report of the Independent Committee on the National Reconnaissance Office ... the Committee on Armed Services, U.S. Senate. Diane Publishing: 2001. Congress investigates whether NRO is a boondoggle. At the time this report was issued, spending on the "stealth satellites" was just ramping up.

The Search for Life on Mars by Malcolm Walter. Perseus: 2000. A slender guide to the subject from a solid publisher.

THE
DAVINCI
CODE
A NOVEL
DAN BROWN
AUTHOR OF ANGELS & DEMONS

The Da Vinci Code

In this section, I'm going to focus on telling you about:

- The best books about *The Da Vinci Code*
- All the news about the movie "The Da Vinci Code"

Books about The Da Vinci Code

Let's start with the books. Here's a handy multi-page table that I made to summarize the strengths and weaknesses of all the books currently available on Amazon.com about *The Da Vinci Code.*

Book title	Author(s)	Fred's comments
Secrets of the Code: The Unauthorized Guide to the Mysteries Behind The Da Vinci Code	Dan Burstein (Editor)	The single most cost-efficient book you can purchase, with an impressively thorough collection of essays about every aspect of *The Da Vinci Code.* I was a bit troubled, though, by the book's excessive even-handedness. Perhaps out of politeness to his contributors, Burstein gives neutral, unjudgmental introductions to even the looniest of his authors. Nevertheless, this is far and away the best of the Code books in terms of value for dollar.
Truth and Fiction in the Da Vinci Code: A Historian Reveals What We Really Know about Jesus, Mary Magdalene, and Constantine	Bart D. Ehrman	A slender volume by a professor of religious studies at the University of North Carolina Chapel Hill who brings the perspective of a "critical historian" to the topic. I loved his list of 10 major errors. I was troubled by his perspective on the Gospels, such as one passage where he suggests that one of the gospel authors was obviously "jazzing up" a story by another

The Da Vinci Hoax: Exposing the Errors in The Da Vinci Code	Carl E. Olson, Sandra Miesel	I remember Sandra Miesel fondly from her a past life as the biographer and frequent collaborator of the late science fiction author Gordon R. Dickson. This book is written from the point of view of Catholics and medievalists who are absolutely outraged by the thesis of *The Da Vinci Code*. The authors know their stuff.
The Truth Behind the Da Vinci Code: A Challenging Response to the Bestselling Novel	Richard Abanes	For Christians who want a clear, concise explanation of why *The Da Vinci Code* is fiction. As Amazon.com reviewer David R. Bess wrote, "This little volume is a breath of fresh air for the layperson who has been suffocated by the Code's academic-sounding arguments."
Breaking The Da Vinci Code : Answers to the Questions Everybody's Asking	Darrell L., Ph.D Bock, Francis J. Moloney	Slender scholarly work that is heavy on discussion of primary sources and philology. Not extremely readable. Best suited for those with a fairly narrow academic focus.
Da Vinci Code Decoded: The Truth Behind the New York Times #1 Bestseller	Martin Lunn	From the author's bio on Amazon.com: "**Martin Lunn** is a recognized expert in the Davidic bloodline and other issues presented in *Da Vinci Code*. He has a masters degree in history and an extensive background in journalism. .... He is also Grand Master of the Dragon Society, founded originally in 1408 by King Sigismund of Hungary." **Awooga! Awooga!** Piercing submarine "dive" alarm, warning that author is probable loon.
De-Coding Da Vinci: The Facts Behind the Fiction of The Da Vinci Code	Amy Welborn	Author is debunker who "holds an MA in Church History from Vanderbilt University." She has editorial review endorsements from the National Review, Spectator Online, and Father Andrew Greeley (Good one!). Ominously, book is "complete with discussion questions and suggestions for further reading in every chapter."

The Da Vinci Code: Fact or Fiction	Hank Hanegraaff, Paul L. Maier	Authors are debunkers and product description on Amazon.com lays the cards on the table: this book "explodes the myths of the book and shows the reliability of Scripture [and] the divinity of Christ... *The Da Vinci Code: Fact or Fiction?* helps you turn debate about the book into an evangelistic opportunity."
Cracking Da Vinci's Code: You've Read the Fiction, Now Read the Facts	James Garlow	Debunkers with a theological agenda. Most disturbing Amazon.com review is the one by Sean who argues that "their primary source of contention to Brown's work is the Bible, which they present as a historical document. ... It is true that Brown offers no concrete data to support his claim about the Bible, but they can neither offer any concrete evidence that the Bible is historical fact. The problem with this book is that it is written by two fundamentalists who have no more evidence than the man they are trying to discredit." Reviewers seem generally in agreement that this book is more poorly documented than many of the other "debunking" essays.
Fact and Fiction in The Da Vinci Code	Steve Kellmeyer	I liked the author's approach of providing page-by-page notes on *The Da Vinci Code,* but unfortunately his stream-of-consciousness musings are those of a debunker with an axe to grind and no great scholarly depth of knowledge. With this book, you can flip through *The Da Vinci Code* and find things to pop off on. Example: Langdon mentions Wicca in Chapter 4. Kellmeyer hammers this one to death: "Wicca does not have any relics. The Wicca religion was invented during World War II by English civil servant Gerald Gardner ... primarily because he liked to walk around in the nude ... [and] commit adultery."
The Da Vinci Deception	Erwin Lutzer	Slender essay by debunker writing for well-known Christian publishing house.

Recommended reading

If you are looking for ammunition to debunk *The Da Vinci Code,* I recommend **The Da Vinci Hoax: Exposing the Errors in The Da Vinci Code**: by Carl Olsen and Sandra Miesel, especially if you are a Catholic. If you are of an evangelical protestant bent, I like Darrell Bock's **Breaking The Da Vinci Code : Answers to the Questions Everybody's Asking**

If you are looking for support for the ideas put forth in *The Da Vinci Code,* I recommend reading Elaine Pagels' books, The Gnostic Gospels and Beyond Belief: the Secret Gospel of Thomas. These are seminal scholarly works that provide a reasonable introduction to the history of the Gnostic Gospels.

If you are simply looking to broaden your understanding, I recommend the Dan Burstein book, Secrets of the Code: The Unauthorized Guide to the Mysteries Behind The Da Vinci Code. It's the best of all the books I read.

"The Da Vinci Code" Movie

The cast

Tom Hanks will play the role of Robert Langdon.

Hanks in "The Terminal"–foreshadowing his role as Robert Langdon, Harvard symbologist?[15]

According to the IMDB Pro STARmeter, Hanks's popularity among Internet movie searchers has been in a bit of a decline in the last couple of years (which merely goes to show that movie fans have short attention spans ... Hanks hasn't lost any of the skills that make him one of the world's greatest actors.)

[15] http://i.imdb.com/Photos/Ss/0362227/TT003.jpg

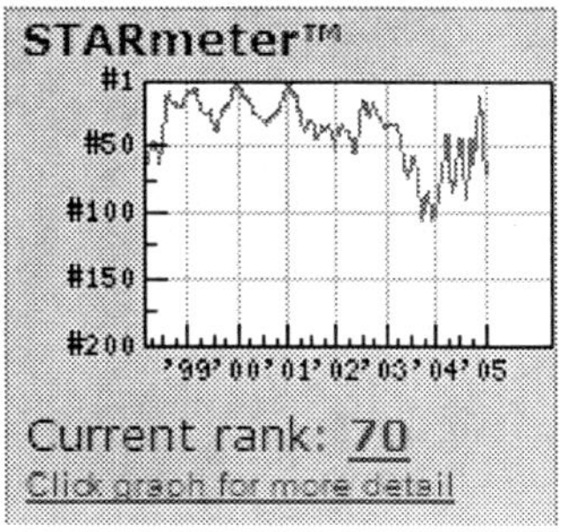
STARmeter™
#1
#50
#100
#150
#200
'99' 00' 01' 02' 03' 04' 05
Current rank: 70
Click graph for more detail

Tom Hanks search rank at the IMDB.[16]

The upward spike at the end of 2004-2005 is related to the announcement of "The Da Vinci Code" movie. Can anyone spell "blockbuster"?

Audrey Tautou has been cast as Sophie Neveu. From this photo, it looks as if she does have some of that loving wiseness that needs to be built into the character (who otherwise spends a great deal of time running around solving puzzles and being outraged at her grandfather).

Tautou in Le Fabuleux destin d'Amélie Poulain", or "Amélie," her biggest U.S. hit.[17]

[16] http://pro.imdb.com/name/nm0000158/graph

[17] http://pro.imdb.com/name/nm0851582/photogallery-ss-4-5

Her IMDB Pro STARmeter shows that Tautou has been a mid-range star with steady progress. This may be her breakout role.

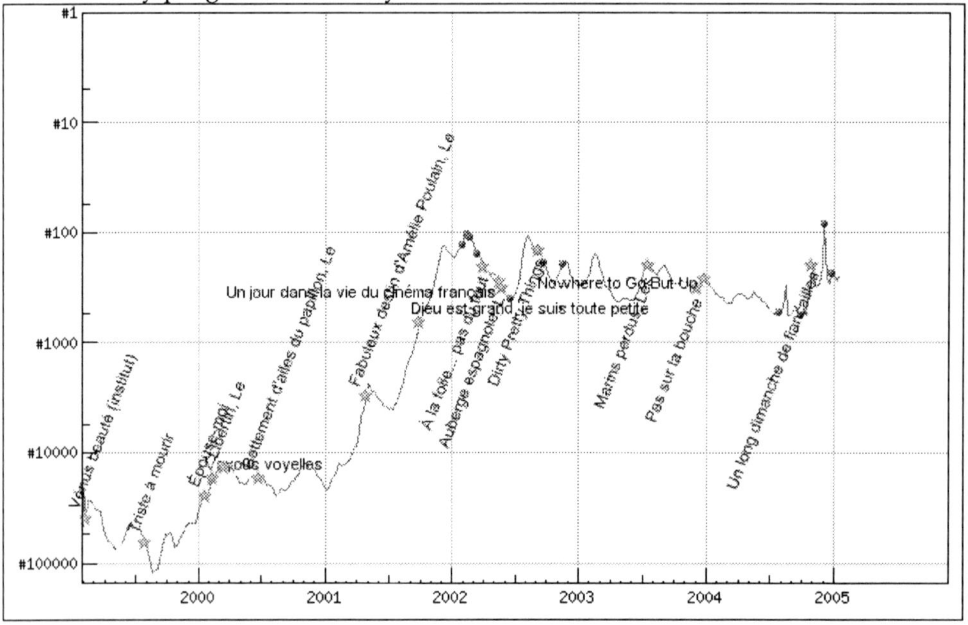
#1
#10
#100
#1000
#10000
#100000
2000
2001
2002
2003
2004
2005
Un jour dans la vie du cinéma français
Dieu est grand, je suis toute petite
Triste à mourir
Marins perdus, Les
Pas sur la bouche
Un long dimanche de fiançailles

IMDB Pro STARmeter with high points of Audrey Tautou's career to date.[18]

Jean Reno has been cast as detective Bezu Fache, one of Langdon's principal antagonists. Reno most recently appeared in the critically well regarded "Hotel Rwanda," and is a familiar action movie bad guy.

[18] http://pro.imdb.com/graph/name/nm0851582/events

Jean Reno as the title character in "Godzilla."[19]

[19] http://i.imdb.com/Photos/Ss/0120685/6

The production

Columbia Pictures owns the rights to produce the movie version. The movie will be shot in 2005 and released on May 19, 2006.

The producer is Brian Grazer.

The director is Ron Howard ("Opie"), director of "Apollo 13."

The first screenwriter of record is Akiva Goldsman. According to the IMDB, he is 'known for "A Beautiful Mind," "I, Robot," and "Batman Forever." A rather ominous list of credits, to which further investigation adds another couple of "Batman" flicks, "Lost in Space," and the movies based on the John Grisham books *The Client* and *A Time to Kill.*

The production designer is Allan Cameron. According to IMDB, his recent credits include "Van Helsing", "The Mummy Returns," "The Mummy," and "Starship Troopers." Pardon me if I am not overly encouraged. The last thing this movie needs is a cartoon-like design.

Cinematographer: Salvatore Totino. According to IMDB, he's only been lead cinematographer a couple of times. He worked with Ron Howard on 2003's "The Missing" and on Oliver Stone's 1999 football film, "Any Given Sunday."

By contrast, the composer is James Horner, an accomplished old hand who is responsible for the scores of more than 145 movies, including "Titanic," "A Beautiful Mind," and "Land Before Time IX: Journey to the Big Water."

WHICH IS MORE IMPORTANT: THE IMAGES OR THE MUSIC?

The combination of a relatively inexperienced cinematographer with a massively experienced composer raises an interesting question about how the producers are investing in the top-line talent. Which is more important for a movie of "The Da Vinci Code," the images or the music?

It looks to me as if they're thinking that the visuals in the movie will be stunning no matter who is the cinematographer: they don't need a top-drawer artiste, just someone who can work well with Howard and get the film in the can. After all, How much talent do you need to make interesting film out of Tom Hanks standing front of the Louvre, the Mona Lisa, and the Madonna of the Rocks?

What makes me nervous is the thought that such beautiful images deserve the utmost artistry in cinematography.

IMDB lists at least three locations where the movie will be shot:

- London, England, UK
- Musée du Louvre, Paris, France
- Paris, France

Hyperlinks to full details about the movie and the key personnel may be found at the IMDB page for the movie, and in the "Information Launchpad," at the end of this book.

Tom Hanks is *Robert Langdon*

Tom Hanks has officially signed for the role of Robert Langdon. Hanks seems to be a good choice to play Robert Langdon. He's great at registering the thoughtful emotions needed for the role ... awe; sensitivity to the sacred female; passionate desire to *know*. At the same time, he ought to be able to do a pretty good job of registering the appropriate levels of plain old *fear* that are needed to drive the thriller aspects of the plot.

Why Tom Hanks?

Ron Howard told *Newsweek* why he liked Hanks:

> "Tom is an exciting actor to watch thinking," Howard was quoted as saying in the latest issue of Newsweek. "We probably don't need his status from a box office standpoint, but he gives Langdon instant legitimacy." [20]

Howard's comments on casting Hanks reveal a lot about what the production team is thinking.

First, they know that they could cast Garfield the Cat™ as Robert Langdon and still make their money back. The movie version of "Da Vinci Code" is, in the immortal words of George Tenet, a "slam dunk."

Second, they regard the Langdon character's "legitimacy" as a potentially troublesome issue. It's a suggestive thought. In what sense could

---

[20] (CNN, November 15, 2004; http://edition.cnn.com/2004/SHOWBIZ/Movies/11/15/film.hanks.reut/)

the character be considered not legitimate? Well, if he comes across as a kook, or as an anti-Christian whack job, the whole movie could fall apart, couldn't it?

After all, what really differentiates the Robert Langdon character from the Robin Williams portrayal of "The Fisher King" as a wild-eyed apparent lunatic? Yes, he's a Harvard symbologist, and we can be sure the movie will remind us of that right away ... but they can only take that so far. In the book, we can hear Langdon thinking, and it's credible because, well, *Dan Brown* seems pretty darned smart. In the movie, we're going to have to spend quite a bit of time watching Tom Hanks think ... so he had better seem smart. It's not clear that, say, Dennis Quaid could be as convincing.

Third, it suggests that they are not thinking sequel. This is a little harder to figure out, because there's already a ready-made prequel (Angels & Demons) and Hollywood surely knows that Brown already has plans for a dozen more Langdon novels (see below, "Into the Future"). Obviously, it's out of the question to imagine a dozen more Hanks movies, so

If Hanks hadn't been available ...

It is a bit of a shame that there won't be an open casting call among past, present, and future stars. Imagine the stunt-casting possibilities.

Madonna as Sophie Neveu (or Robert Langdon?)

John Wayne as Langdon: "Wa'al, ma'am ..."

Clint Eastwood as the Catholic Church. "I know what you're thinking. Were there twelve disciples, or were there actually thirteen? Well, to tell you the truth, in all this excitement, I've kinda lost track myself. But being as this is the Pope, the most powerful religious leader in the world, and he can have Opus Dei blow your head clean off, you've got to ask yourself one question: Do I feel lucky? Well, do ya, punk?"

Jeff Daniels and Jim Carrey as Silas and the Teacher ("Dumb and Dumber").

More on the cast

French actress Julie Delpy angled for the role of cryptologist Sophie Neveu in an interview on World Entertainment News Network in December

2004, saying "Da Vinci is mine!" But according to The Guardian, she didn't have much luck.

> According to the French broadsheet Le Journal du Dimanche, the producers went to Paris to audition French actors and have come up with a shortlist of six. They are: Sophie Marceau, Audrey Tautou, Virginie Ledoyen (Leonardo DiCaprio's love interest in The Beach), Amira Casar (recently seen in the UK in Catherine Breillat's Anatomy of Hell), Judith Godrèche (previous credits outside France: The Man in the Iron Mask and Ridicule) and Linda Hardy, a former Miss France.[21]

The article viewed in its native French is not without a certain piquancy.[22]

28 CULTURE

Six Françaises en quête du Da Vinci Code

Hollywood prépare activement le tournage d'un film inspiré par le best-seller de Dan Brown.

Le Louvre attend les caméras

"Six Francaises en quête du Da Vinci Code" translates as "Six Frenchwomen in quest for *The Da Vinci Code.*" The French text goes on to say that the actresses were flown off to LA to meet Tom Hanks and do screen tests. Quel dommage! Not a bad trip, eh?

If you had your way about the cast...

Some clever movie fans at Imagine Casting LLC have come up with a way for fans to vote on casting for their favorite real (and hypothetical) movies. Here are the top results for "The Da Vinci Code." As of November 17 (shortly after the appearance of the first Tom Hanks rumors). http://imaginecasting.com/imagine/topPicks.php?Movie_ID=54

---

[21] http://film.guardian.co.uk/news/story/0,12589,1393880,00.html

22http://www.pressdisplay.com/pressdisplay/pageview.aspx?issue=25202005011600000000001001&page=28

Character	Robert Langdon	Total Votes: 184	Fred's comments
1.	Paul McGann	14 % (25)	Who?
2.	David Duchovny	9 % (16)	Snore. X-Files is so over.
3.	Aaron Eckhart	8 % (15)	Who?
Character	**Sophie Neveu**	**Total Votes: 172**	
1.	Sophie Marceau	20 % (35)	Why is it necessary that the role of Sophie Neveu should be played by a French woman? What's wrong with Meg Ryan, or Cher?
2.	Rachel Weisz	15 % (25)	When I saw her in "Runaway Jury," I didn't think "there goes the great-great-granddaughter of Jesus Christ."
3.	Kate Beckinsale	12 % (21)	Famous for plastic surgery = daughter of Christ? I think not.
Character	**Bezu Fache**	**Total Votes: 147**	
1.	Jean Reno	54 % (80)	Good guess!
2.	Tcheky Karyo	11 % (16)	Who?
3.	Alfred Molina	5 % (8)	Good, especially if he's got some of that Doc Ock anger burning a la "SpiderMan 2".

Character	Leigh Teabing	Total Votes: 143	Fred's comments
1.	Jim Broadbent	20 % (29)	For some reason, I saw Leigh Teabing as more of a thin Roddy MacDowell type.
2.	Sean Connery	13 % (19)	At first I thought too robust, but then I realized that could make the "unveil" more plausible.
3.	Ian McKellen	12 % (17)	Gandalf? Wrong wizard.
Character	**Collett**	**Total Votes: 113**	
1.	Vincent Cassel	27 % (31)	Who?
2.	Michael Vartan	12 % (14)	My wife says this "Alias" star is a must. He does have a wavering quality that feels right for the role.
3.	Gary Oldman	11 % (12)	Doesn't he have a TV series now?
Character	**Silas**	**Total Votes: 141**	
1.	Paul Bettany	28 % (39)	Who?
2.	Crispin Glover	10 % (14)	I can't stop thinking about "Back to the Future."
3.	John Malkovich	7 % (10)	Too predictable.
Character	**Bishop Aringarosa**	**Total Votes: 134**	
1.	Alfred Molina	19 % (25)	Yes – a brilliant bit of stunt casting!
2.	Geoffrey Rush	16 % (22)	Who?
3.	Gabriel Byrne	14 % (19)	Too good-looking for a Bishop.

Character	Remy	Total Votes: 116	
1.	Ben Kingsley	22 % (25)	Very close … this would mean we have to give BK an Oscar-worthy death scene, which I'm not sure is merited in terms of the plot.
2.	John Turturro	16 % (18)	
3.	Gary Oldman	7 % (8)	Another bit of stunt casting.
Character	**Jacques Sauniere**	**Total Votes: 130**	
1.	Ian McKellen	28 % (36)	Gandalf is exactly the right association for the modern audience. Gets the message across that he's a good guy before he ever says a word on-screen.
2.	Ian Holm	15 % (20)	Bilbo Baggin *is* Jacques Sauniere?[23] I think not.
3.	Anthony Hopkins	15 % (19)	Remember, we have to see him naked in the pivotal "ritual" scene.

Anticipation for the movie is building steadily

Amazon.com IMDB Pro service offers a great feature called MovieMeter, which ranks searches related to "The Da Vinci Code" against all other movie searches. As the graph shows, interest has been building steadily, and reached the top 100 late in 2004.

[23] http://pro.imdb.com/name/nm0000453/photogallery-ss-0-0

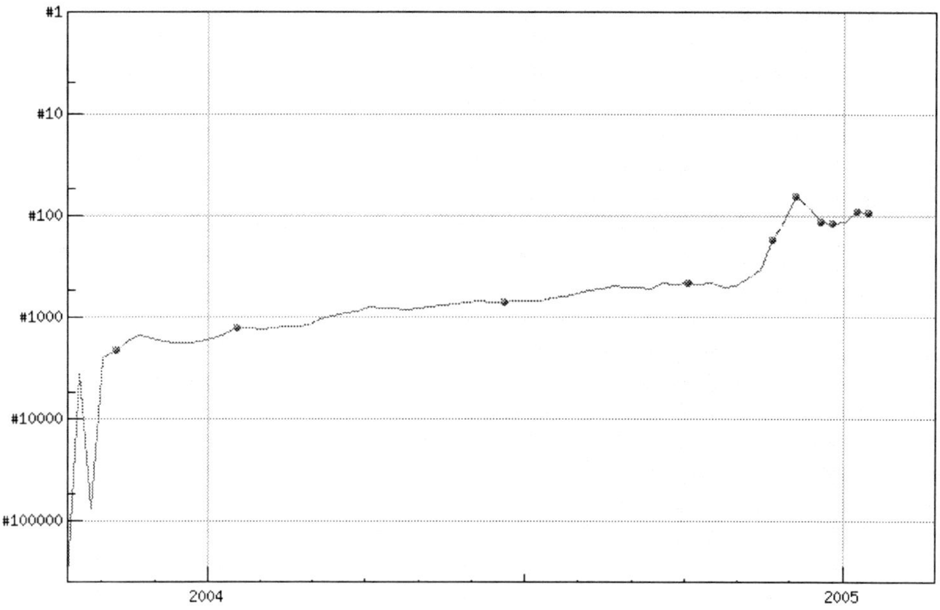
#1
#10
#100
#1000
#10000
#100000
2004
2005

Don't defame the albinos!

The National Organization For Albinism And Hypopigmentation (NOAH) issued a stern warning against portraying the albino character Silas as a red-eyed psychopath.

> [T]he organization looks ahead with concern to 2005 as director Ron Howard and Imagine Entertainment begin work on the movie version of the best-selling fictional novel 'The Da Vinci Code.'
>
> NOAH has written and called Imagine Entertainment several times beginning in February 2004 to express concerns about Silas, a murderous monk depicted in the novel as an albino. So far Imagine has not acknowledged NOAH' s concern nor made any comment about how they plan to depict Silas. "Ron Howard and Imagine can make a big difference for people with albinism by continuing the trend away from a hack device if they adjust the Silas character to not be an evil albino" said Mike McGowan, NOAH president. "Over the years the stereotyping and misinformation foisted on the albinism community by filmmakers who don't take the time to learn the facts about albinism does real harm to real people."

> According to a list compiled by UCSF dermatologist Dr. Vail Reese, for his website www.skinema.com, 12 motion pictures released in the 1980s featured an evil albino, 20 did so in the 1990s, and 24 after 2000. In 2004 the only person with albinism in a notable film released in the United States was Noi, the hapless adolescent in the Icelandic film, 'Noi Albinoi.'
>
> NOAH is concerned that fictional novels and movies depict people with albinism so inaccurately that the fiction overwhelms reality. "One huge problem with 'The Da Vinci Code' is how Silas is described with red eyes," McGowan said. "That's a myth. Most often in people with albinism the eyes are light blue or even hazel." Though their eyes are a normal color, many with albinism have impaired vision. McGowan points out that it is ironic that movies dating back to 'The Firm,' and 'Lethal Weapon,' have made people with albinism into sharpshooters. NOAH argues that the evil albino is a hackneyed plot device used repeatedly by filmmakers depicting people with albinism as being only wicked . NOAH believes that the absence of positive albino characters in motion pictures contributes to misinformation about the condition and stereotyping and discrimination against people with albinism.
>
> Albinism is an inherited condition that affects about 1 in 17,000 people in the United States. It occurs in all races and ethnic groups. In addition to noticeably reduced pigment in the skin and hair, most people with albinism have uncorrectable low vision because of a problem in the development of the retina. Many people with albinism are considered legally blind. However, with appropriate vision rehabilitation people with albinism hold productive jobs in a wide variety of professions.

I was tempted to make fun of this, but this organization offers some good facts to back them up. Fortunately, Silas is not a continuing character, so in the case of *The Da Vinci Code* the problem is a self-limiting one.

The Solomon Key

The Solomon Key was once rumored to be the title of Dan Brown's next novel. In 2005 his publisher, Doubleday, stated that it could not confirm *The Solomon Key* as the title of the next book. On the other hand, Doubleday did not rule it out as a title, either, so in my mind, *The Solomon Key* is still the most likely title. At this point, only Dan Brown knows for sure!

There's still a place where you can sign up to pre-order *The Solomon Key* at Amazon.com:

http://www.amazon.com/exec/obidos/tg/detail/-/B0006H92F6/

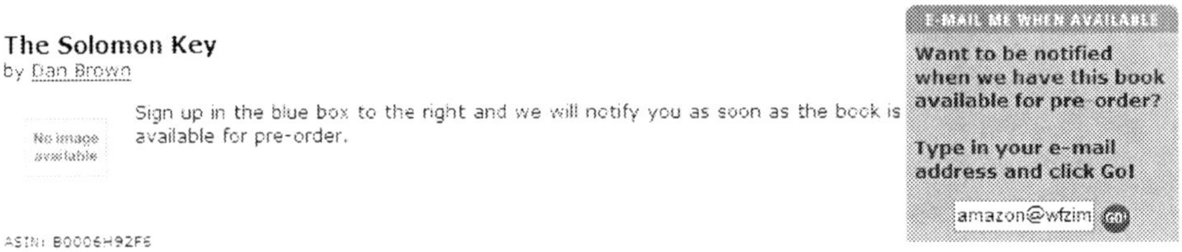
The Solomon Key
by Dan Brown
No image available
Sign up in the blue box to the right and we will notify you as soon as the book is available for pre-order.
ASIN: B0006H92F6
E-MAIL ME WHEN AVAILABLE
Want to be notified when we have this book available for pre-order?
Type in your e-mail address and click Go!
amazon@wfzim
GO!

When exactly *will the next novel be published?*

Here's what I know:

- As of May 15, 2006, no publication date had been released.
- As of May 15, 2006, there have been no public statements, to suggest that the manuscript is completed.
- Brown's UK publisher, Transworld, confirmed in spring 2006 that the book would not be published before 2007.
- Six months from announcement to release date would be pretty typical. By way of comparison, the July 16, 2005 release date for JK Rowling's Harry Potter and the Half-Blood Prince was announced on Dec. 22, 2004.
- As of May 15, 2006, there was absolutely no sign of a publication date.

Bearing all this in mind, my estimate is that the book will be released in fall 2007.

> **Tip:** take anything you read about release dates with a giant grain of salt, unless it's in a press release from Doubleday with a specific date attached.

Where will the story begin?

From one of Brown's comments on his website, it sounds as if *The Solomon Key* will begin with Robert Langdon right where Dan Brown left him at the end of *The Da Vinci Code.*

> My next novel will be another Robert Langdon adventure (picking up, in fact, where The Da Vinci Code left off).[24]

Does he mean this literally, or will there be an "offstage" gap between the events in *Da Vinci* and *The Solomon Key,* as there was a one-year gap between the events in *Angels & Demons* and *The Da Vinci Code*?

My guess is that since Brown went out of his way to emphasize that the story picks up where *The Da Vinci Code* left off, he does indeed mean that literally, which suggests that at the beginning of *The Solomon Key,* Robert Langdon will be in Paris, at the site of the famous "inverted pyramid" in the Louvre where he receives the novel's final revelation about the nature of the Holy Grail.

Brown clearly prefigures that Sophie Neveu will not be a permanent relationship for Langdon with a novelist's trick of emphasizing the strong and immediate emotional connection between Sophie and her brother when they meet at Rosslyn Chapel. Although Langdon spends a few "enchanted evenings" with Sophie in Paris, they don't seem to be on a trajectory for the picket fence and swing sets in the backyard. So the logical next step for Langdon is to return home alone. My guess is that he won't be taking a direct flight!

---

[24] http://www.danbrown.com/meet_dan/faq.html

Langdon en route from Paris to Dulles

Brown has stated that *The Solomon Key* will be set in Washington, D.C.

> For the first time, Langdon will find himself embroiled in a mystery on U.S. soil. This new novel explores the hidden history of our nation's capital.[25]

So it sounds as if some unforeseen event will interfere with Langdon's return to Harvard. And from Brown's previous remarks, it sounds as if Langdon will be wandering into the location shooting for "National Treasure" (the 2004 thriller starring Nicolas Cage and the back of the dollar bill).

The Freemason connection

In October 2004, *The New York Times* summarized comments about *The Solomon Key* by Stephen Rubin, president of Doubleday:

> The new book's primary focus will be the Freemasons, the secretive fraternity that has included some of the nation's founding fathers, and it will be set in Washington, D.C.
>
> In first discussing the subject of the book last spring, Brown mentioned that the architecture of Washington is rich in symbolism, something that he is using in the novel.[26]

Almost all the news stories about *The Solomon Key* that appeared in the months from November 2004 to January 2005 were basically recycling this story.

Learning about the Freemasons

Dan Brown gave this fabulously helpful advice in an interview with BookBrowse.com:

> There is so much written on the Freemasons that it's difficult to know where to begin. Having researched the Freemasons in depth (both through books and interviews

---

[25] http://www.danbrown.com/meet_dan/faq.html

[26] New York Times, October 30, 2004.

> with Masons), I will warn readers that the vast majority of books written about the brotherhood are inaccurate. Many books are written by non-Masons and are therefore hypothetical and, in many cases, paranoid conspiracy theory. For accurate information on the brotherhood, you should read only those titles written by Masons (or former Masons). That is, unless you are convinced the brotherhood is hiding something.[27]

My advice is that as usual, it's best to start with the most credible sources, typically official publications and writings by academics with "real" credentials, i.e. tenured Ph.D. professors at major research universities.

The Google Scholar service is a reasonable place to start:

http://scholar.google.com/scholar?q=freemason&ie=UTF-8&oe=UTF-8&hl=en&btnG=Search

Be warned that many of the Google Scholar articles are from professional publishing companies that require payment.

Another good place to start is your local university library.

Numerology important in The Solomon Key

In the excellent BookBrowse interview, Brown mentions that a numerological cult will play a key role in *The Solomon Key.*

> [T]he book also drops a hint as to the identity of another ultrasecret numerology sect that fascinates me, but I can't reveal their name here without ruining much of the surprise of the next book.[28]

I already wish I didn't know this, because frankly I don't place a lot of stock in numerology. I'm good at arithmetic and at word games, so it all seems awfully easy to manipulate.

---

[27] http://tinyurl.com/4ogtg

[28] http://tinyurl.com/4ogtg

The Original Da Vinci Code Challenge

Greg Taylor of The Daily Grail has written a fine book called Da Vinci in America: Unlocking the Secrets of Dan Brown's "The Solomon Key."[29] In it, Taylor provides fans with instructions on how to solve the Original Da Vinci Code Challenge[30] at www.danbrown.com. (A complete list of questions may be found at http://liskot.org/~daniela/da_vinci_code.html). If you successfully solve the clues, you get some fascinating clues about *The Solomon Key.*

Is there no hope for the Widow's son?

Dan Burstein (*Secrets of the Code*[31]) explained the meaning of the "Widow's son" this way in a May 2004 press release:

> "Look closely at the text of The Da Vinci Code's dust jacket and you will find select letters that stand out in very slightly bolded type," says Burstein, whose SECRETS OF THE CODE is the most comprehensive, and the only secular guidebook available to The Da Vinci Code. "You have to look carefully and you may not see it at first. In fact, you may need a magnifying glass. But once you find these slightly bolded letters and string them together, they clearly spell out an intriguing question: 'Is there no help for the widow's son?'
>
> "This question is tinged with allusions and meanings. It is a reference to the Book of Enoch, one of the most unusual of the Apocrypha. It is also a reference to Mormon traditions, Masonic traditions, and to science fiction writer Robert Anton Wilson, whose Illuminati series includes a novel entitled, Widow's Son."
>
> "'Is there no help for the widow's son?' was the title of a now famous talk given before a Mormon audience in 1974 that sought to establish a connection between Freemasonry and the founder of the Church of the Latter Day Saints, Joseph Smith. The talk was secretly tape-recorded and has been widely circulated, much to the chagrin of many in the Mormon Church. Many Masonic lodges have 'widow's son' events to this day. Mormon temples are often decorated with Masonic symbology. I

[29] http://www.amazon.com/exec/obidos/tg/detail/-/0975720007

[30] http://www.randomhouse.com/doubleday/davinci/index-ctc.html

[31] http://www.amazon.com/exec/obidos/tg/detail/-/1593150229

> believe the sequel to The Da Vinci Code will involve a Mormon-Mason treasure hunt through the U.S., with Robert Langdon back to lead us through the interpretation of all these symbols."

It's amazing that Dan Brown was able to influence his book's cover art to such an extent prior to the overwhelming success of *The Da Vinci Code.* From all accounts, the normal procedure is that the design team goes off in a corner then returns to present the author with something of *a fait accompli.* This is further evidence of the genius-level marketing effort associated with *The Da Vinci Code.*

Apparently the story about the relationship between Mormons and Masons will come front and center. The article "Is there no help for the widow's son?" which apparently started this whole thread may be found at:

http://www.xmission.com/~country/reason/widowson.htm

To make a looong story short, the author suggests that there were remarkable similarities between the history of Masonry and the history of Mormonism. Enoch ("seventh in the line of patriarchs from Adam") was a founder of Masonry, while Joseph Smith, founder of Mormonism, "was named Enoch, even by God." Enoch buried two sacred treasures–the story of the Tower of Babel, and the Secret Mysteries he had inherited from Adam , including the sacred name of Godin a hill called Moriah. Doughty Masons protected the Mysteries, including one dude called Hiram Abif, or Hiram, the widow's son. While being slain by bad guys who were after the treasure, Hiram cried out, "Oh Lord, My God, is there no hope for the widow's son"–which has, ever since, been a distress call for Masons. The first four words of the slogan–"Oh Lord, My God"–were Joseph Smith's last words in his death by lynching on June 27, 1844.

Loopy stuff. We'll see whether this plays a role.

Kryptos

The Original Da Vinci Code Challenge analyzed by Greg Taylor in *DaVinci in America* also includes a clue that leads readers to the famous statue *Kryptos* at CIA headquarters in Langley, Virginal. It seems reasonable that this beautiful work of art will figure in *The Solomon Key.*

Kryptos by James Sanborn

The CIA web site has a thorough explanation of the history of *Kryptos*[32]. In a nutshell, the sculpture contains four separate codes. The first three have been broken; as of May 15, 2006, the second had not.

Elonka's *Kryptos* page [33] is a good starting place for further investigation.

Here is the solution to the first code, posted by computer scientist Jim Gillogly to the cypherpunks mailing list[34]

- `Between subtle shading and the absence of light lies the nuance of iqlusion. Keys: KRYPTOS, PALIMPSEST.`

---

32 http://www.cia.gov/cia/information/tour/kryptos_code.html

33 http://elonka.com/kryptos/

34 http://www.ideosphere.com/fx/lists/fx-discuss/1999/0930.html

- It was totally invisible. How's that possible? They used the earth's magnetic field. x The information was gathered and transmitted undergruund to an unknown location. x Does langley know about this? They should: it's buried out there somewhere. x Who knows the exact location? Only WW. This was his last message. x Thirty eight degrees fifty seven minutes six point five seconds north, seventy seven degrees eight minutes forty four seconds west. ID by rows. Keys: KRYPTOS, ABSCISSA

- Slowly, desparatly [sic] slowly, the remains of passage debris that encumbered the lower part of the doorway was removed. With trembling hands I made a tiny breach in the upper left-hand corner. And then, widening the hole a little, I inserted the candle and peered in. The hot air escaping from the chamber caused the flame to flicker, but presently details of the room within emerged from the mist. x Can you see anything? q Keys: three columnar transpositions.

The Original Da Vinci Code Challenge includes a question drawing attention to the initials "WW" in the second paragraph, which presumably stand for "William Webster," the director of the Agency at the time the sculpture was created.

The Challenge also draws attention to the latitude and longitude coordinates 38 57 6.5 N, 77 8 44 W, but with the first number altered to 37. Wired magazine reports that"[Brown has] said that he may reveal the reason in future books."[35]

The last paragraph is a quotation from Howard Carter's book about the opening of King Tut's tomb. So far, no clues about why this passage was selected, or whether Tut will feature in *The Solomon Key*. (I can see Steve Martin in the movie version.)

Part 4 of the code is as follows:

```
                        ?OBKR
UOXOGHULBSOLIFBBWFLRVQQPRNGKSSO
TWTQSJQSSEKZZWATJKLUDIAWINFBNYP
VTTMZFPKWGDKZXTJCDIGKUHUAUEKCAR
```

You can bet Kryptos will be in *The Solomon Key*.

[35]"Solving the Enigma of Kryptos", Kim Zetter, Jan 21, 2005. http://www.wired.com/news/culture/0,1284,66334,00.html

WHAT HOWARD CARTER SAW NEXT

Here is what Howard Carter saw next:

> It was all I could do to get out the words, "Yes, wonderful things." Then, widening the hole a little further, so that we both could see, we inserted an electric torch.
>
> Chapter VI
>
> Preliminary Investigation
>
> ...Surely never before in the whole history of excavation had such an amazing sight been seen as the light of our torch revealed to us. ...
>
> Gradually the scene grew clearer, and we could pick out individual objects. First, right opposite to us—we had been conscious of them all the while but refused to believe in them—were three great gilt couches, their sides carved in the form of monstrous animals, curiously attenuated in body, as they had to be to serve their purpose, but with heads of startling realism... Next, on the right, two statutes caught and held our attention; two life-sized figures of a king in black, facing each other like sentinels, gold kilted, gold sandaled, armed with mace and staff, the protective sacred cobra upon their foreheads.
>
> ...
>
> ... Presently it dawned upon our bewildered brains that in all this medley of objects before us there was no coffin or trace of mummy ... The explanation gradually dawned upon us. ... What we saw was merely an antechamber. Behind the guarded door there were to be other chambers, ... and in one of them, ... in all his magnificent panoply of death, we should find the Pharaoh lying.[36]

E Pluribus Unum

The Challenge draws attention to the famous slogan on the Great Seal of the United States, "e pluribus unum," or "out of many, one." To get started on the history of the Great Seal, I recommend the official explanation from

[36] *The Tomb of Tut-Ankh-Amen,* Howard Carter and A,C. Mace (New York: Cooper Square, 1963) volume 1, p. 96.

the Department of State.[37] Perhaps the most interesting item in there is that President Franklin D. Roosevelt was responsible for the most recent changes in the Seal.

> We see the seal design almost every day, both the obverse and the little-noticed reverse, as it passes through our hands on the $1 bill. In 1935, the Department of the Treasury sent President Roosevelt a new design for the bill, incorporating the obverse and reverse of the Great Seal. After approving it rather routinely, the President changed his mind, scratched out his signature, and inked in several significant changes. He switched the obverse and reverse and added "The Great Seal" under a rough outline of the pyramid and "of the United States" under an even rougher sketch of the eagle, and initialed the whole "FDR." Upon receipt, Treasury's Bureau of Engraving and Printing duly noted "Received by the Engraving Division June 26, 1935," and revised the model.

The State Department's explanation.

Mona Lisa's *Oeil Droit*

Greg Taylor reports that the final question in the Challenge asks the reader to click on the Mona Lisa's "Oeil Droit," or right eye. Taylor speculates that this may have something to do with the right eye of Horus, the Egyptian god of the sun. We'll find out when *The Solomon Key* is released! It's looking better and better all the time.

[37] http://www.state.gov/www/publications/great_seal.pdf

The Solomon Key: Chapter-by-Chapter Analysis

The Solomon Key: *Chapter 1*

Detailed analysis of this chapter will be incorporated in this *Update* soon after the publication of *The Solomon Key.* Remember that you are entitled to a free PDF update of this book when you present proof of purchase directly to Nimble Books via e-mail to updates@nimblebooks.com.

The Solomon Key: *Chapter 2*

The Solomon Key: *Chapter 3*

The Solomon Key: *Chapter n*

Into the Future with Dan Brown

Dan Brown 2025

Dan Brown is a pretty young guy ... it's quite reasonable to expect that he has another twenty or thirty years left in his writing career. What can we expect from those years?

Get used to Robert Langdon

Brown says he has plans for a more than a dozen more Robert Langdon books.

> Will your next book also feature Robert Langdon?
>
> Indeed. I intend to make Robert Langdon my primary character for years to come. His expertise in symbology and iconography affords him the luxury of virtually endless adventures in exotic locales. ***Currently, I have rough sketches for almost a dozen Robert Langdon thrillers set in mysterious locations around the globe.*** [emphasis added][38]

Success and continual improvement?

Brown's shown great improvement over his first four books. Interestingly, I believe the greatest improvement came in books 2 & 4, when he switched from science fiction to art history. In some respects, *Digital Fortress* and *Deception Point* are simply unsuccessful science fiction. The word has two meanings here. First, the books are, in my opinion, not fully successful as stories. Not that they're not good and enjoyable, simply that they don't rise to the level of flawlessness that keeps us rereading great novels like *The Andromeda Strain* and *Tinker, Tailor, Solider, Spy.* Second, the books do not describe successful science fictional innovations. Instead, in each case, the big new thing that is the mainspring of the plot *fails to happen.* Free cryptography is not unleashed on the world, and Mars is not found to have life.

---

[38] http://tinyurl.com/4ogtg

By contrast, I found *Angels & Demons* and *The Da Vinci Code* to be highly successful as mystery novels with an art historical and theological setting and a near-future science fiction background (the High-Speed Civil Transport, anti-matter, etc.). The $64,000 question is whether I would feel the same way if I knew more about art history and theology. Also, in each case, the big secret that is the mainspring of the plot *is* successfully revealed. We find out what the Camerlengo and the Illuminati were up to, and we find out the true meaning of the Holy Grail.

It'll be interesting to see what happens with the next couple of novels. If Brown can continue to improve on the Robert Langdon series, his potential is unlimited.

Brown seems to be a hard worker, and not especially vulnerable to the dreaded "Brain Eater's Disease" that has left many successful authors writing on as shadows of their former selves, cranking out formulaic imitations of their best work.

A Hall of Fame trajectory?

In sports writing it's commonplace to compare the early careers of rising superstars with their illustrious predecessors. In some of the more statistically minded sports such as baseball, elaborate analysis has been done to project whether today's stars will make into the Hall of Fame.[39]

Will Dan Brown be in the fiction writers' Hall of Fame? He'll never win a Nobel Prize for Literature, but if it were up to the publishing industry, he would already have earned it. *The Da Vinci Code* is a break-out season to end all break-out seasons … like Bobby Bonds hitting100 home runs in his fourth season, or LeBron James's Cavaliers going 82-0.

Let's compare Dan Brown's first four books to the first four books by some of his favorite writers.

> What are your 10 favorite books —and why?
>
> Of Mice and Men (John Steinbeck) —Simple, suspenseful, and poignant. Better yet, the first paragraph of every chapter is a master class in writing effective description.
>
> Kane and Abel (Jeffrey Archer) —I was amazed how well Archer handled the long time spans without ever losing

---

[39] See, for example, http://www.baseball-reference.com/leaders/hof_monitor.shtml.

the narrative pulse. The ultimate novel of sibling rivalry.

Plum Island (Nelson DeMille) —He remains the master of substance, wry humor, and controlled point of view.

The Bourne Identity Series (Ludlum) —Ludlum's early books are complex, smart, and yet still move at a lightning pace. This series got me interested in the genre of big-concept, international thrillers.

Dan Brown	**John Steinbeck**	**Nelson DeMille**	**Sidney Sheldon**	**Robert Ludlum**
Digital Fortress (1998)	*Cup of Gold* (1929)	*The Hammer Of God* (1974)	*The Naked Face* (1970)	*The Scarlatti Inheritance* (1971)
Angels & Demons (2000)	*The Pastures of Heaven (1932)*	*The Smack Man..* (1975)	*The Other Side of Midnight.* (1973)	*The Osterman Weekend* (1972)
Deception Point (2001)	*The Red Pony* (1933)	*By The Rivers Of Babylon* (1978)	*A Stranger in the Mirror.* (1976)	*The Matlock Paper* (1973)
The Da Vinci Code (2003)	*To A God Unknown* (1933)	*Cathedral.* 1981)	*Bloodline* (1977)	*The Rhinemann Exchange* (1974)

Sheldon enjoyed great success with his first few books, and they've sold a ton of copies over the years. *The Red Pony* was still assigned in English class back in the Stone Ages when I went to high school. *The Ostermann Weekend* is still a darned clever book. But in this list, from both a financial point of view and from a fame point of view, *The Da Vinci Code* stands alone. It's hard to imagine that Dan Brown will ever write another book that is more famous or sells more copies. If he does, he deserves a special seat in the Hall of Fame.

What to hope for

Let's hope Dan Brown reads more genre fiction.

> Until I graduated from college, I had read almost no modern commercial fiction at all (having focused primarily on the "classics" in school). In 1994, while vacationing in Tahiti, I found an old copy of Sydney Sheldon's Doomsday Conspiracy on the beach. I read the first page… and then the next…and then the next. Several hours later, I finished the book and thought, "Hey, I can do that." Upon my return, I began work on my first novel-- Digital Fortress -- which was published in 1996.[40]

There's not a single work of genre fiction in his list of 10 favorite books (above).

Since, as we discussed in a preceding chapter, Brown is *de facto* writing in the science fiction and mystery genres, let's hope that Brown makes the time to read some of the genre greats like Michael Crichton, John Le Carre, George R.R. Martin, Dorothy Sayers, and Larry Niven. An appreciation of the intelligence and subtlety of characterization and thought that goes into the very best of genre fiction would, I believe, substantially improve Brown's work.

[40] http://www.danbrown.com/meet_dan/faq.html

Dan Brown's Hidden Guide to Selling a Novel

Brown summarized his approach to writing fiction in a terrific interview in the Internet Writers' Journal.

> **What advice do you have for beginning writers hoping to get published?** Only one piece of advice: Write a commercial manuscript. ... I was given a number of great tips on writing saleable manuscripts, and for anyone interested, I've posted them on-line.

The address he gave in that IWJ interview is no longer valid, but the document is still available in a "hidden" location on Brown's website. The document is stored at http://www.danbrown.com/tips.htm.

The tips are well worth inspecting, because they offer an amazing glimpse into the mind of a tremendously successful author.

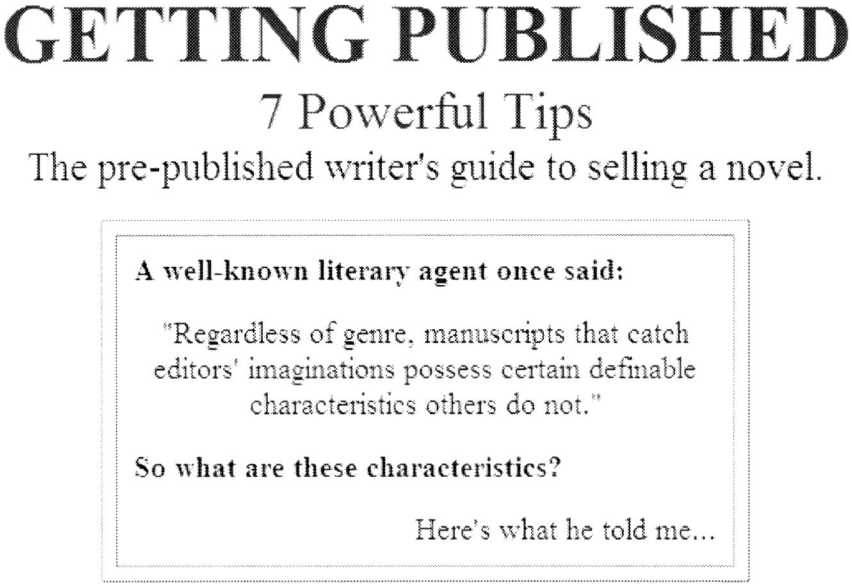

GETTING PUBLISHED

7 Powerful Tips

The pre-published writer's guide to selling a novel.

A well-known literary agent once said:

"Regardless of genre, manuscripts that catch editors' imaginations possess certain definable characteristics others do not."

So what are these characteristics?

Here's what he told me...

The first screen of the hidden guide.

Brown builds a terrific checklist using the following touchstones:

- A sole dramatic subject
- Setting, setting, setting
- In and out scene building
- Creating tension,
- Specifics
- Information Weaving
- Revision

Completely worth reading for any aspiring novelists!

Dan Brown witness statement in Da Vinci Code case

(Reproduced with minor editorial enhancements from the version published in the *Times* of London.)

IN THE HIGH COURT OF JUSTICE CHANCERY DIVISION INTELLECTUAL PROPERTY BETWEEN:

1) MICHAEL BAIGENT

2) RICHARD LEIGH

Claimants

THE RANDOM HOUSE GROUP LIMITED

Defendant

FIRST WITNESS STATEMENT OF DAN BROWN

I, DAN BROWN, care of Random House, Inc., 1745 Broadway, New York, NY 10019, United States of America, **WILL SAY** as follows:-

I. I am the author of four novels, Digital Fortress (1998), Angels & Demons (2000), Deception Point (2001), and The DaVinci Code (2003). In this statement I make reference to all four of my books, and I assume that the reader has some familiarity with my books but, in particular, has read The Da Vinci Code.

2. I live and work in the United States. I am a graduate of Amherst College and of Phillips Exeter Academy, where I also spent time as an English teacher before turning to writing full time.

Introduction

3. My father is a teacher emeritus at Phillips Exeter Academy and also has published more than a dozen well-known academic texts used around the world. He received the Presidential Award for excellence in mathematics teaching. Both of my parents are musicians, and both have served as church choir masters. My mother has a master's degree in sacred music and was a

professional church organist. My father sings and was an actor in musical theatre. To this day, both continue to sing and are members of a Symphony Chorus that will be touring Europe this summer. This love of music, like many things my parents loved, was inherited by me. When I was at Amherst I was very interested in music composition and creative writing. I also loved languages.

4. I grew up on the campus of Phillips Exeter Academy, where my father was a teacher. By chance, the school has a very strong tradition of writing and has a number of famous writers as alumni, including John Irving, Gore Vidal, Daniel Webster, and Peter Benchley. It is also known for the strictness of its regulations and code of conduct, especially with respect to plagiarism. I notice from the school's website that plagiarism is still considered a "major offence", exactly as it was in my day.

5. While at Phillips Exeter and Amherst College, I pursued advanced writing courses and was published in school literary magazines. At Exeter, I chose "creative writing" as my senior project. At Amherst, I applied for and was accepted to a special writing course with visiting novelist Alan Lelchuk.

6. I studied English and Spanish at school. During my high school summers, I travelled to Spain on two exchange programs and fell in love with the country. In 1985, while I was still a student at Amherst College, I spent the school year abroad in Seville, Spain, where I enrolled in a two semester art history course at University of Sevil1e. This art course covered the entire history of World Art- from the Egyptians to Jackson Pollock. The professor's slide presentations included images ranging from the pyramids, religious icons, renaissance painting and sculpture, all the way through to the pop artists of modem times.

7. This course opened my eyes to the concept of art as "communication" between artist and viewer. The artist's language, I learned, was often symbolism and metaphor, and the professor's revelation of the hidden meanings of the violent images in Picasso's "La Guemica" has stayed with me to this day, as has his passion for the absolute pain of Michelangelo's Pieta. The course covered many other works that resonated with me as a young man, including the horror of Goya's Saturn Devouring His Son and the bizarre anamorphic sexual nightmares of Bosch's Garden of Earthly Delights. I was surprised by the unexpected "dark quality" of Leonardo daVinci's The Last Supper. I remember the professor pointing out things I hadn't seen

before, including a disembodied hand clutching a dagger and a disciple making a threatening gesture across the throat of another.

8. The course was a chronology of art history, and I took a specific interest in the renaissance masters of Bernini, Michelangelo, Raphael, and Leonardo da Vinci.

9. Both the art course and the country itself had a great influence on my writing. In fact, I was so taken with the architecture of Seville that, ten years later, when I wrote my first novel (Digital Fortress), I set much of the action in Seville. There are scenes in the Cathedral of Seville, atop the Moorish tower La Giralda, the ancient alleyways of Barrio Santa Cruz, Parque Maria Luisa, and the Alfonso XIII. I was taught early on at Phillips Exeter that "one must write what one knows". Like many aspects of my life, scenes from my childhood, my relationship with my parents and family, my student years, and my time in Spain all later emerged in my books.

10. I took piano lessons since the age of six and wrote music throughout high school and college. Once I had finished college in May of1986, I focused my creative energies on song writing. I left home and moved to Los Angeles, the heart of the song writing industry, where I had limited success in music and paid my rent by working as an English teacher at Beverly Hills Prep School. Over the course of the ten years after college, I wrote and produced four albums of original music. I met my wife, Blythe, through the National Academy of Songwriters, where she was the Director of Artist Development. Blythe, like me, loved art. She also was a very talented painter. Despite the Academy's best efforts to promote me, my music career never really took off.

11. In 1993, Blythe and I vacationed together to Tahiti. I remember reading a book called The Doomsday Conspiracy, by Sidney Sheldon. Up until this point, almost all of my reading had been dictated by my schooling (primarily classics like Faulkner, Steinbeck, Dostoyevsky, Shakespeare, etc.), and I'd read almost no commercial fiction at all since The Hardy Boys as a child. The Sheldon book was unlike anything I'd read as an adult. It held my attention, kept me turning pages, and reminded me how much fun it could be to read. The simplicity of the prose and efficiency of the storyline was less cumbersome than the dense novels of my schooldays, and I began to suspect that maybe I could write a "thriller" of this type one day. This inkling, combined with my musical frustrations at that time, planted the seed that perhaps I could write books for a living.

187 Men to Avoid

12. As an Easterner, I felt like a fish out of water in Los Angeles. I lived in a low- rent "artists", apartment complex, whose hallways overflowed with unusual individuals-aspiring rock stars, male models, drama queens, and stand-up comics. Amazed by this new world, I thought it might be fun to compile a list of some of the more bizarre sightings. Over the course of a few days, I wrote a list and called it: 187 Men to Avoid. Blythe thought the list was hilarious. She quickly wrote several literary agents and included a portion of the list. To my astonishment, I immediately got calls from a number of agents, including George Wieser, who told me he had already spoken to Putnam Books and could get me $12,500 for manuscript. Having faced disappointment in the music industry, this quick success in publishing surprised and encouraged me. I agreed to sell the manuscript and chose to use a female pseudonym (albeit a pretty obvious one, Danielle Brown).

13. 187 Men to Avoid was published in August 1995 by Berkley Publishing Group. Around the time of publication of 187 Men to Avoid, my new literary agent, George Wieser, came across an article I had written for the Phillips Exeter Magazine entitled: "Goodness and Knowledge on the Sunset Strip". The article was a humorous look about the travails of a "preppy geek from New Hampshire" who had been transplanted to Los Angeles. George told me over lunch that he had seen the article, loved my writing style and "power of observations". He strongly encouraged me to write a novel. He told me that he had been in the business a long time and "knew a novelist when he saw one". Although I still had aspirations of writing a mainstream novel that was as fun to read as the one I'd read in Tahiti, I was still focused on song writing and felt I should give my music career a fair chance to catch on. In addition, I had no idea what I would write about.

Digital Fortress (published 1998)

14. The "big idea" for my first book came to me by chance. In around 1995 I was on the campus of Phillips Exeter Academy in New Hampshire. At that time, the U.S. Secret Service came to campus and detained one of the students claiming he was a threat to national security. As it turned out, the student had sent a private email to a friend saying how much he hated

President Clinton and how he thought the president should be shot. The Secret Service came to campus to make sure the boy wasn't serious. After some interrogation the agents decided the student was harmless, and not much came of it. Nonetheless, the incident really stuck with me. Email was brand new on the scene, and like most people, I assumed email was private. I couldn't figure out how the secret service knew what these students were saying in their email.

15. I began doing some research into where organizations like the Secret Service get their intelligence data, and what I found out astonished me. All roads led to a powerful intelligence agency larger than the CIA, but which few Americans knew existed - The National Security Agency (NSA) - home to the United States' eavesdroppers and code breakers.

16. I continued researching NSA more in depth. A particularly influential book, at the time, was James Bamford's The-Puzzle Palace (D.26), which although dated, is still one of the seminal books on the covert world of America's premier intelligence agency, describing how the NSA pulls in intelligence data from around the globe, processing it for subversive material.

17. The more I learned about this ultra secret agency and the fascinating moral issues surrounding national security and civilian privacy, the more I realized it could be a great backdrop for a novel. I remember Blythe commenting that life seemed to be trying to tell me something. The music industry was clearly rejecting me, and the publishing industry seemed to be beckoning. The thrill of being a published author (187 Men To Avoid), combined with George Wieser's words of encouragement, my newfound fascination with NSA, and the vacation reading of Sidney Sheldon's The Doomsday Conspiracy, all had begun to give me confidence that I could indeed write a novel. I quite literally woke up one morning and decided to write a thriller that delved into NSA. That's when I started writing Digital Fortress.

18. NSA is home to the world's most potent computers as well as some of the most brilliant cryptographers, mathematicians, technicians, and analysts. Digital Fortress is about a brilliant female cryptographer (Susan Fletcher) who works for NSA and the adventures she and her partner (David Becker, a linguist and lecturer) have in parallel throughout the book.

19. So, I had my "big idea" for the book. The novel explored what I consider to be a fine line between civilian privacy and national security. My first reaction had been that the security methods used in. the U.S. were a gross invasion of civilian privacy. When I found out, however, that the NSA helped thwart terrorist attacks, my view changed. Initially, I had been indignant that the NSA was reading emails. But subsequently I realized their work constituted a fascinating moral grey area.

Researching and Writing Digital Fortress

20. I have followed a very similar approach to researching and then writing each of my four novels. The first step is to select a theme that I find particularly intriguing, this is generally the "big idea". Because my novels are so research intensive, they take up to two years to write, if I am going to stay focused on a two year project, it is imperative that I remain excited about the subject matter. Therefore, I choose a subject which is not black and white, but rather contains a grey area. The ideal topic has no clear right and wrong, no definite good and evil, and makes for great debate. The one aspect of writing that is by far the most difficult is staying motivated over the entire time that it takes to research and write a novel. I keep myself interested by writing about things that interest me. I have some favourite subjects, which I wove into the Digital Fortress story once I had my "big idea" in place. For me, the "must have" themes include codes, puzzles and treasure hunts, secretive organizations, and academic lectures on obscure topics.

21. For me, writing is a discipline, much like playing a musical instrument; it requires constant practice and honing of skills. For this reason, I write seven days a week. So, my routine begins at around 4:00 AM every morning, when there are no distractions. (The routine of writing early began while I was writing Digital Fortress; I had two daytime teaching jobs to pay the bills, and the early mornings were my only free time; I found I liked working at that hour, and though I no longer teach, I have remained faithful to that routine.) By making writing my first order of business every day, I am giving it enormous symbolic importance in my life, which helps keep me motivated. If I'm not at my desk by sunrise, I feel like I'm missing my most productive hours. In addition to starting early, I keep an antique hour glass

on my desk and every hour break briefly to do push-ups, sit-ups, and some quick stretches. I find this helps keep the blood (and ideas) flowing.

22. I did all of the research and background reading for Digital Fortress. I found that much of the data on the NSA was unclassified and in the public domain. There are a number of intelligence sources who have written extensive white papers on NSA. For the background reading on computers, viruses, codes and cryptography, I found helpful Bruce Schneiers's famous book Applied Cryptography: Protocols, Algorithms, and Source Code in C. (D.56)

23. After the basic reading is done and my theme or "big idea" is in place, I start researching and writing in earnest. I erect the frame on which to build the plot I try to sketch out the overall shape of the story. When I taught creative writing, I told my students they could not select the veneer for the cupboards before they'd poured the foundation for their houses.

24. Because my novels are very "location driven", I always select a series of key settings that I want to use in the novel (e.g., NSA, the Seville Cathedral, La Giralda, etc.). The hero of Digital Fortress, David Becker, finds himself on the run through a landscape of ancient Moorish towers, Sevillian barrios, and the Cathedral of Seville. Much of the early work is to place these locations in a workable sequence such that the characters can move from one to the next in a logical manner.

25. In trying to craft a suspenseful framework, I decided to throw Becker into a world he did not understand. I also took him away from the heroine, his fiancée, Susan Fletcher. A lot of the suspense of this novel derives from wondering if these two will be reunited. In general, my plots drive my need for specifics (such as the precise vehicle a character will use to move from point A to B) rather than vice versa.

26. Although Digital Fortress was very much my first attempt at writing a compelling thriller (and there is plenty I would do differently if I were writing it today), it contains some themes that I return to in all of my books.

27. With the NSA in place, I had the right backdrop to include my favourite theme (which is in all of my books) --codes and treasure hunts. My books are all "treasure hunts" of sorts. In each of my books, the treasure is an object. In Digital Fortress it is a gold ring; in Angels & Demons, it is antimatter; in Deception Point, it is a meteorite; and in The Da Vinci Code, it

is the Holy Grail. I think people enjoy this sort of quest, especially trying to stay a step ahead of the hero by deciphering the clues along the way.

28. I have always been interested in secrets and puzzles. They played a large part in my life growing up in New Hampshire. I grew up in a house of mathematics, music and language; codes and ciphers really are the fusion of all of those things. In our house there was no television, and I used to spend hours working out anagrams and crossword puzzles. My father has a passion for brain puzzles, and I have inherited this passion. My father inspired my early passion for codes by creating elaborate treasure hunts for our birthdays and Christmas. On Christmas morning when most kids would find their presents under the tree, my siblings and I might find a treasure map with codes and clues that we would follow from room to room and eventually find our presents hidden somewhere else in the house. If properly solved, these clues would lead us to a secret location in our house -or sometimes even lead us to ride around town on our bicycles from one clue to the other, before finding where the presents were hidden. It was wonderful fun - for me codes and treasure hunts have always been a passion.

29. This early love of codes means that there is a short jump to another favourite subject, namely secrets and secret organizations. All four of my books have the thread of secrecy. All deal with secretive topics - covert spy agencies, conspiracy theories, classified technologies, and secret history.

30. An example of what I mean by "secret history" appears in the opening and closing chapters of Digital Fortress I describe how David Becker, the hero, signs his messages to his lover, Susan Fletcher, the NSA cryptographer, with the words "without wax". This vexes Susan, much to David's delight. Only at the end of the book do I decode the words and reveal a nugget of history:

"During the Renaissance, Spanish sculptors who made mistakes while carving expensive marble often patched their flaws with cera - 'wax'. A statue that has no flaws and required no patching was hailed as a 'sculpture sin cera' or a 'sculpture without wax'. The phrase eventually came to mean anything honest or true. The English word 'sincere' evolved from the Spanish sin cera 'without wax'. David's secret code was no great mystery - he was simply signing his letters 'Sincerely.' Somehow he suspected Susan would not be amused."

(Digital Fortress, Corgi, page 508)

31. I remember at the time getting a kick out of the combination of the hidden code and the "nugget" of history. As I explain below, this idea of revealing interesting pieces of information so that the novel becomes a "thriller as academic lecture" really took off in my second book, Angels & Demons. In my first book, I was still paddling around trying to work out how to write a book and also to find out what I liked to write about. In Digital Fortress there is, for example, a little history, about Galileo, but this is merely window dressing.

Editing of the manuscript of Digital Fortress

32. Once I had stitched together the whole story, I asked Blythe to read the completed manuscript. I also gave a copy to my parents. I incorporated some of their comments and then sent the manuscript to my then agent, George Wieser, in New York. To my great surprise, George called to tell me the first editor who read the manuscript had made an offer to buy it. Digital Fortress was signed to a publisher - St Martin's Press -in only about 20 days after I finished it.

33. I am very careful about what I send to my publisher. I work a manuscript as far as possible before showing it to anyone (rather than submitting rough drafts). By the time my editor sees pages, I have rewritten and polished them many times. For this reason, the first draft normally provokes few suggestions for substantive changes. My editor will take a look at the overall structure of the book and how the whole thing hangs together. He or she might say, for example, "these three chapters in the middle are very slow, it might be a good idea to combine them"; or "this is a very good point, you should expand".

34. Once I get the feedback from my editor, I completely re-writes and re-submit the manuscript. My editors for Digital Fortress were Thomas Dunne and Melissa Jacobs. They both described my submitted manuscript as "exceptionally clean" and requiring very little editing. One thing they did do was suggest that I change the name from "The Worm" to "Digital Fortress', which was the name I had chosen for the unbreakable code described in the book, Once the editor is finished with the manuscript, it is sent to copy editors and fact checkers to review grammar and accuracy.

35. Once my work on the novel is finished, I may take a vacation, in the early days, funds permitting, or start thinking about the next book. Of course, at this point -Digital Fortress was published in 1998 - I was an unknown, unpublished author. I was still teaching English, and some Spanish, to make a living. Money was tight, but we had enough to travel, something Blythe and I both love, and we decided to visit Rome. I had either finished or almost finished Digital Fortress, I am not sure of the time line.

Angels & Demons (published 2000)

36. Sometime after completing Digital Fortress, I had several other ideas in development but hadn't yet decided on a direction. I had enjoyed writing about the NSA, computers, technology and, of course, "secrets". I had read about CERN - Conseil European pour la Recherche Nucleaire - which is the world's largest scientific research facility. It is located in Geneva, Switzerland and employs over 3,000 of the world's top scientists. In addition, CERN is the birthplace of the World Wide Web. Also CERN was researching antimatter, an enormously volatile substance which I found fascinating. I read that CERN was regularly producing small quantities of antimatter in their research for future energy sources. Antimatter holds tremendous promise; it creates no pollution or radiation, and a single droplet could power New York City for a ful1 day. With fossil fuels dwindling, the promise of harnessing antimatter could be an enormous leap for the future of this planet. Of course, mastering antimatter technology brings with it a dilemma: this science could be used for good or evil; to power the world or create a deadly weapon. I thought this would make a good plot element for a novel.

37. I still had not decided on the main topic for my new novel when Blythe and I visited Rome. We were beneath Vatican City touring a tunnel called il passetto -- a concealed passageway used by the early Popes to escape in event of enemy attack. It runs from the Vatican to Castle Saint Angelo. According to the tour guide, one of the Vatican's most feared ancient enemies was a group of early scientists who had vowed revenge against the Vatican for crimes against scientists like Galileo and Copernicus. History had called them many things - the enlightened ones, the Illuminati, The Cult of Galileo. I added the Illuminati to my mixing pot of ideas.

38. Upon my return home, I started looking into the Illuminati, and what I found was material for a great thriller. I read conspiracy theories on the Illuminati that included infiltration of the British Parliament and U.S. Treasury, secret involvement with the Masons, affiliation with covert satanic cults, a plan for a New World Order, and even the resurgence of their ancient pact to destroy Vatican City. However, as much as I liked the idea of the Illuminati (and using Rome as a dramatic stage), I still had all the material on CERN and antimatter, which I did not want to go to waste. The question was how to combine the two ideas.

39. Both in prep school and college, I had studied science, including that of Galileo, modem cosmology, and Darwin. I also attended church camp and was trying to reconcile science and religion in my own mind. My parents' opposing views (my father an agnostic mathematician and my mother a religious church musician) made for an interesting childhood. I grew up surrounded by the paradoxical philosophies of science and religion, and though I wanted to believe in Christianity, as I got older and studied more science, I had a hard time reconciling the two. I once asked a priest how I could believe both the "the Big Bang" and the story of Genesis, and the "matter of faith" type response I received never answered my questions. At college, I completed a cosmology course that included a section on Copernicus, Bruno, Galileo, and the Vatican Inquisition against science. Science and religion was a very large part of my life from grade school all the way through college, and I wanted to make them harmonious on a personal level.

40. So, I began reading books on science and religion, including The God Particle (D.47), The Tao of Physics, The Physics of Immortality, The Quark and the Jaguar, and others. The recurring theme that excited me was the idea that science and religion were now dabbling in common areas. These two ancient enemies were starting to find shared ground, and CERN was at the forefront of that research.

41. This was how I ended up writing Angels & Demons - a science vs. religion thriller set within a Swiss physics laboratory and Vatican City. The grey area that interested me was the ongoing battle between science and religion, and the faint hope of reconciliation between the two. This was my "big idea" and my "grey area". Much more so than with Digital Fortress, I

thought I had hit on 'something that really would keep my attention for the next two years.

42. Looking back at my notes and the first pages of a proposal for Angels & Demons (D.243), I see from my 'Partial Bibliography that at the time I was reading three broad categories of books - those concerning science v. religion (The God Particle (0.47) etc.); those concerning symbology (Dictionary of Symbols, by Chevalier (D.30)); and books about The Illuminati and the Masons (e.g., The Illuminati, by McKeown; Encyclopaedia of Freemasonry, by Mackey). I used the description 'Partial Bibliography' as a lot of my research comes from conversations, research trips, online sources, etc. - essentially sources that are hard to cite - as well as books. I found some of the science v. religion books so interesting that I mentioned them by name in Angels & Demons as a tribute, much like that I paid to several texts in The Da Vinci Code. In both novels, the books appear on a, character's book-shelf.

Robert Langdon

43. Robert Langdon is an amalgam of many people I admire. In the early 1990's, I first saw the art work of John Langdon. John is an artist and philosopher, a close friend of my father and, I think, one of our true geniuses. He is most famous for his ability to create "ambigrams" - words that read the same both right side up and up side down (see, for example, his book Wordplay (D.46)). John's art changed the way I think about symmetry, symbols, and art - he looks at art from different perspectives. I was so impressed by the artwork of John Langdon that I commissioned him to create an album cover for my new CD of music (called Angels & Demons), which dealt with many of the religious themes that already interested me. John did the artwork, and the CD was released in 1999 with John's ambigram on the cover. Later, when I published a novel of the same name, Simon & Schuster used the same ambigram on the hardcover edition.

44. John and his name as part of the inspiration for the protagonist of Angels & Demons (Robert Langdon) who also appears in The Da Vinci Code and in my next, as yet unpublished, book. John also created the ambigrams used in Angels & Demons. I commissioned him to create ambigrams for the word "illuminati", as well s the Illuminati diamond-the fusion of the

elements, earth, air, fire and water, which represents the fusion of science and religion historically, and features in Angels & Demons (Corgi, page 520).

45. As a tribute to John Langdon, I named the protagonist Robert Langdon. I thought it was a fantastic name. It sounds very "New England" and I like last names with two syllables (Becker, Langdon, Sexton, Vetra, et al). Every character has his purpose, and with Langdon I wanted to create a teacher. Many of the people I admire most are teachers --my father is the obvious figure from my own life. My father had introduced me to the artwork of M.C. Escher (he lectured worldwide on symmetry and M.C. Escher). (I mentioned the Mobius Strip -a twisted ring of paper, which technically possessed only one side - in Angels & Demons, Corgi, page 133.) John Langdon is also a teacher.

46. Another teacher I greatly admire is Joseph Campbell, a religious historian; symbologist, and partial inspiration for my character. Roughly around about this time, I watched a TV program, "The Power of Myth", in which Bill Moyers interviewed Joseph Campbell about the deeper meanings of symbols and art from many different cultures and creeds. I recall being impressed by Campbell's open-minded and unthreatening delivery, especially when he spoke about controversial topics like myths and untruths in religion. I recall thinking that I wanted my character Robert Langdon to have this same open-minded tone.

47. In choosing what characters to include in a novel, I select characters who have sets of skills that help move the plot along and also permit me to introduce information. Robert Langdon is a symbologist and art historian for the same reason that the heroine in Digital Fortress is a cryptologist; these characters help decipher clues and teach the reader.

48. For my heroine in Angels & Demons, I chose the name Vittoria Vetra. Vittoria is a scientist - a Marine Biologist who specializes in the new field of Entanglement Physics. I've spoken to physicists about this new field and the incredible experiments they are now running, some with the hope of proving' God exists. Some experiments have been run in hopes of proving unseen communication between separate animal entities. One such experiment I read about involved a sea turtle egg. Sea turtle eggs are unique in that a nest of hundreds of eggs will all hatch at the exact same moment. In an effort to determine how this took place, scientists removed one egg and placed it in a terrarium halfway around the globe with a video camera. As

soon as the eggs in the nest started hatching, the eggs on the other side of the globe started hatching simultaneously. I find these kind of experiments fascinating. I wanted a character who could credibly share this kind of information with my readers.

49. Angels & Demons is the first Robert Langdon novel - The Da Vinci Code was the second. It was a real joy for me to write, and a breakthrough in terms of finding my own style (although I can only say that with hindsight). I intend to make Robert Langdon my primary character for years to come. His expertise in symbology and iconography affords him the luxury of potentially limitless adventures in exotic locales. It was also a book in which Blythe could be more involved, as she has a great love of art and art history. In Angels & Demons I was able to really develop the "nuggets" of information idea that I had started to play with in Digital Fortress. In that book I found the history behind the phrase "without wax" fascinating, and with this new book there was a lot more to play with. I thought, with the right background, story and characters, this could make for a lot of fun for both me, in researching and writing the book, and hopefully for any readers of the book.

50. Angels & Demons, like all my books, weaves together fact and fiction. Some histories claim the Illuminati vowed vengeance against the Vatican in the 1600's. The early Illuminati - those of Galileo's day- were expelled from Rome by the Vatican and hunted mercilessly. The Illuminati fled and went into hiding in Bavaria where they began mixing with other refugee groups fleeing the Catholic purges --mystics, alchemists, scientists, occultists, Muslims, Jews. From this mixing pot, a new Illuminati emerged. A darker Illuminati. A deeply anti Christian Illuminati. They grew very powerful, infiltrating power structures, employing mysterious rites, retaining deadly secrecy, and vowing someday to rise again and take revenge on the Catholic Church. Angels & Demons is a thriller about the Illuminati's long awaited resurgence and vengeance against their oppressors. But most of all, it is a story about Robert Langdon, the Harvard symbologist who gets caught in the middle. Much of the novel's story is a chase across modem Rome - through catacombs, cathedrals, piazzas, and even the Vatican's subterranean Necropolis.

51. Although there are some similarities with my first book - the murder, the chase through a foreign location, the action taking place all in 24 hours,

the codes, the ticking clock, the strong male and female characters, the love interest - I think the real advances I made in the second novel were as follows.

Advances in Angels & Demons

(a) The idea of the thriller as academic lecture

52. I tried to write a book that I would love to read. The kind of books I enjoy are those in which you learn. My hope was that readers would be entertained and also learn enough to want to use the book as a point of departure for more reading. When I was researching the book, I would learn things that fascinated readers. Rome was a location that allowed me to immerse myself in the history of religion, art, and architecture. For example, I visited the Pantheon. The docent talked to me about the history of the building - specifically its use as a pagan temple before being converted to Christian church. We talked about Constantine's role in converting the pagans (including the Mithraics and the cult of Sol Invictus). Although I was familiar with Constantine, I learned about the cult of Sol Invictus, which was new to me, in particular its role in the choice of some of the dates of Christian holidays. This led to the section in Angels & Demons where Langdon is giving a lecture to his class about

Christianity and Sun Worship. He mentions Sol Invictus and Christianity borrowing from the previous religions.

(b) Hidden information and secret societies

53. Angels & Demons, like The Da Vinci Code after it, features a secret society. I had played with the subject of secretive organizations and hidden

information in the first book in a high-tech setting. In Angels & Demons, however, I found far more interesting aspects to include. For example, the design of the Great Seal on the U.S. dollar bill includes an illustration of a pyramid - an object which arguably has nothing to do with American history. The pyramid, I learned, was actually an Egyptian occult symbol representing a convergence upward toward the ultimate source of illumination: in this case, an all seeing eye. The eye inside the triangle is a pagan symbol adopted by the Illuminati to signify the brotherhood's ability to infiltrate and watch all things. In addition, the triangle (Greek Delta) is the scientific symbol for change. Some historians feel the Great Seal's 'shining delta' is symbolic of the Illuminati's desire to bring about 'enlightened change' from the myth of religion to the truth of science. All of this research and reading about the Illuminati led me also to learning more about Freemasons. This research was something I would come back to when I started to write and research The Da Vinci Code and also the book which I am currently writing.

54, Another group I read about while doing research for Angels & Demons was The Knights Templar. In Angels & Demons, the Templar Crusades play a major role in the back-story of one of my main characters (the Hassassin). I found Templar history fascinating. My recollection is that I had considered including more material on the Templars but decided to set it aside because I could not make all of Templar history fit into the tight framework of this novel.

55. I have asked myself why all this clandestine material interests me. At a fundamental level my interest in secret societies came from growing up in New England, surrounded by the clandestine clubs of Ivy League universities, the Masonic lodges of the Founding Fathers, and the hidden hallways of early government power. I see New England as having a long tradition of elite private clubs, fraternities, and secrecy - indeed, my third Robert Langdon novel (a work in progress) is set within the Masons. I have always found the concept of secret societies, codes, and means of communication fascinating. In my youth I was very aware of the Skull & Bones club at Yale. I had good friends who were members of Harvard's secret "finals" clubs. In the town where I grew up, there was a Masonic lodge,

and nobody could (or would) tell me what happened behind those closed doors. All of this secrecy captivated me as a young man.

(c) Codes and treasure hunts

56. Angels & Demons built on the writing devices I first used in Digital Fortress. In my first book, the cracking of the code is what accelerates the reader through the pages. In Angels & Demons, I moved away from the straight binary codes into the much more interesting device of clues wrapped up in poems or riddles. The snippets of verse in Angels & Demons are useful tools for releasing information and moving the plot to the next stage. One challenge when "presenting the reader with a complicated code is to control the flow of information so the overall mystery is not overwhelming. Finding a plot device that enables me to dole out information in bite size pieces is helpful. In Angels & Demons, I accomplished this by delivering the code in short snippets of verse, which enables the reader a chance to stay one step ahead of Langdon. Langdon, as a teacher, symbologist and art historian, satisfies dual prerequisites for my hero - that of being a credible teacher and also of being knowledgeable enough to decipher the clues in the artistic treasure hunts I create.

(d) The plot and the writing

57. I think that the plot and writing of Angels & Demons is better than that in Digital Fortress. In this second novel, I laid down a very strict outline of what was going to happen in this book and worked hard to stay on track while fleshing out the story.

58. I tried to write a book that I would love to read. I wanted every single chapter to compel the reader to turn the page. I was taught that efficiency of words is the way an author respects his readers' time, and so I trimmed the novel heavily while I was writing. In Digital Fortress, the action takes place within twenty four hours, and I specifically set out to do that again in Angels & Demons. I compressed the plot and action to intensify the pace of the read, and I tried to keep the reader abreast of where the characters were physically, at all times. That seems to help the reader's feeling that he is right

there the entire time. In addition, I tried to end every chapter with a cliff-hanger.

59. All of my books have a very similar style, and I believe it to be the elements of this style (e.g. doling out information slowly) to which my readers react. All of my novels use the concept of a simple hero pulled out of his familiar world and thrown into a world that he (or she, in Deception Point) does not understand. I use strong female characters; travel and interesting locations; a romance between a man and woman of complementary expertise; a ticking clock (all my novels are set in 24 hours). Structural elements are consistent in every book. I think that it is not so much what I write which is compelling but how I say it. I must admit, however, that I did not realize this until my first three novels became huge bestsellers after The Da Vinci Code. The hard part of writing a novel is not the ideas but rather the nuts and bolts of the plot and language and making it all work.

Researching and writing Angels & Demons

60. Examining religion, art, and architecture was exciting to me. I loved researching these subjects; as did my wife, Blythe. Although I had researched Digital Fortress entirely on my own, for this new book Blythe became my research assistant. This was wonderful. We were able to work together as husband and wife; I now had a sounding board and a travel partner on research trips. Although Blythe's main interest and expertise was art, I. did ask her for help researching specifics on scientific topics like Galileo, the Big Bang, particle accelerators, etc. She also served as a first pass set of eyes for new sections I was writing.

61. Architecture, art, sculpture, and religion are all intertwined, and nowhere more so than in Rome and Vatican City. Once I started to look at artwork for inclusion in the story, I began to focus on particular artists. I knew Bernini had had problems with the Church, for example, his sculpture, The Ecstasy of St. Teresa, which I mention in the book (Angels & Demons, Corgi, page 375), had been controversial. I think that this may have been the trigger for using Bernini in Angels & Demons. I had studied Bernini in Seville and knew a lot about his paintings and work. I was intrigued by the concept that Bernini's artwork might contain hidden messages; I had learned

in art history classes that artists like Bernini (and Da Vinci), when commissioned to create religious art that may have been contrary to their own beliefs, often placed second levels of meaning in their art.

62. As the novel's Author's Notes says, all of the works of art, tombs, tunnels, and architecture in Rome are entirely factual. It took me two separate trips to Rome to locate what I needed. Blythe and I walked miles, took hundreds of photos, and explored the city using all kinds of guidebooks, maps, and tours. The second trip I went over with an art specialist who had ties inside the Vatican. The Vatican has a staggering collection of Renaissance masters such as Michelangelo, Raphael, and Bernini. We spent a week in Rome, and our contact facilitated our gaining special access to the Scavi, access to the unclassified sections of the Vatican archives, as well as our seeing the Pope, both at a mass and in his audience hall.

63. Unfortunately, I did not get access to the Vatican secret archives. There are only a few American scholars who have been allowed into the secret archives; Many of the books inside have been there for hundreds of years, and some have never been seen. I have read that there are four miles of shelves in the Vatican secret archives, and I became captivated by the prospect of what might be kept down there. Before my first visit, I had petitioned for access to certain documents within the Vatican Archives. Not at all surprising to me, my request was denied. Nonetheless, our contact there generously arranged for us to see several restricted areas of the Vatican, including the Necropolis (the city of the dead buried beneath the Vatican), St. Peter's actual crypt (which we learned is not where most people think it is), and some perilous sections of the roof high above the Basilica; all of which featured in Angels & Demons.

Simon & Schuster

64. After our trip to Rome, I had completed an outline for Angels & Demons, including a grand finale at CERN, which ultimately I did not use. St. Martin's Press (SMP, my publisher for Digital Fortress) wanted to buy Angels & Demons, but I had been frustrated by their lack of promotional effort on my behalf. I had taken matters into my own hands. I spent my own money on publicity. I booked more than a hundred radio interviews, doing

several a day for months. Despite good reviews, a very newsworthy/timely topic, and all of my grassroots efforts, the novel sold poorly. I decided that I would change publishing houses. I got an offer from Simon & Schuster, who wanted to buy Angels & Demons based on my outline and promised me a much larger publicity campaign.

65. Because Simon & Schuster had purchased my book in advance, 1 now was writing knowing that 1 had a publisher. I was encouraged because Simon & Schuster said they were extremely excited by Angels & Demons. They promised to give the book considerably more publicity and support than my previous publishers. Their proposed publicity included a much larger print run (60,000), advertising in major newspapers, web advertising, a 12 city tour, an e-book release, and other exciting prospects.

66. Unfortunately, when the book came out, my print run was slashed down to 12,000 copies with virtually no publicity at all. I was once again on my own and despite enthusiastic reviews, the novel sold poorly. Blythe and I were heartbroken as we had put so much work into this book. Once again, we took matters into our own hands, booking our own signings, booking our own radio shows, and selling books out of our car at local events.

67. At this point, my motivation was running thin. (I was still teaching to make ends meet, and I had made little money on Angels & Demons. I still owed Simon & Schuster another novel (I had signed a 2 book deal, with Simon & Schuster having an option on a third), and so I kept going in hopes that my sales would pick up or that one of the novels would be optioned and turned into a movie. At the time, that was a big financial incentive. I did receive numerous offers for the film rights to Angels & Demons, but I turned them down as they were not enough money and not with major studios.

68. This was not an easy time financially. I remember that we were forced to literally sell books out of our car at low profile publishing events. The few readers who read Angels & Demons had gone wild for it, and Blythe and I really believed we had something - if we could only get it to a critical mass of readers. The store where we buy most of our books, The Water Street Bookstore in Exeter New Hampshire, was hand selling my books, but the superstores still did not even know my name. Doing our own publicity and self-funding a book tour was expensive and exhausting. I was seriously considering not writing again. I learned a lot about publicity during this time, none of it very encouraging. I was told that the window of opportunity

in book publishing was only a few weeks and that an author needed to reach a critical mass of readers very quickly after release, or the bookstores would return his books to the publisher to make room for the next round of new books. This is why large scale, coordinated launches are needed to make a success of most books. I realised I could not do it alone, no matter how hard I tried,

Deception Point (published 2001)

69. As I said, this period around 1999 was a very difficult time for me, but I remained hopeful. I was exhausted from the research and writing of such a complicated religious thriller, and I felt like I needed a break from symbols and art history. Even though I had lots of viable material left over from all of my research on religion/art/Rome and the Templars etc. I felt like I needed a change of pace. I decided to write what I later termed a "palate cleanser". After writing about the covert National Security Agency and the clandestine brotherhood of the Illuminati, I found myself hard pressed to come up with a more secretive topic. Fortunately, I had recently learned of another US intelligence agency, more covert even than the National Security Agency. This new agency, The National Reconnaissance Office (NRO), figured prominently in my third novel, Deception Point.

70. The research I had completed for the first book, Digital Fortress; was a good starting point for the third book. I had a lot of information on national security, technology, funding and other government departments. At the time, the press had also been commenting on NASA's string of failures and the feasibility of private aerospace companies taking over NASA's role.

71. This debate gave me my "big idea". I became very interested in the question of whether it made sense for my tax dollars to fund trips to Mars while the very school in which I was teaching could barely afford an art teacher. Then again, could we as human beings really give up our quest for discovery in space? Deception Point centred on issues of morality in politics, human progress, national security, and classified technology. The book explored organizations such as NASA and the NRO. The crux of the novel was the link between NASA, the military, and the political pressures of big budget technology.

72. The novel was a thriller about a meteorite discovered in the Arctic - a discovery that turns out to have profound political ramifications for an impending presidential election. The set up gave me a chance to debate and explore topics of morality in politics and science.

73. Of course, there is a twist in the tale, as there is in all my books. Like its predecessors, Deception Point incorporates my usual elements - a secretive organization, a love story, a chase, and plenty of academic lecture. At the heart, however, my books are all essentially treasure hunts set within a 24 hour period.

Researching and writing Deception Point

74. Unfortunately for Blythe, the technological subject matter of Deception Point did not interest her much. She helped research some of the geology and glaciology, the architecture of the White House, Air Force One, etc., but she served more as a first pass editor and sounding board.

Editing and promotion of Deception Point

75. After the disappointment of the sales of Angels & Demons, I was nervous about the prospects for Deception Point. Simon & Schuster assured me they were going to "build me" as an author and that publicity for my new novel would be better. Unfortunately, it was not.

The Da Vinci Code (published 2003)

76. Halfway through writing Deception Point I began to think that maybe I had made a mistake with this palate cleanser. I was feeling bored by the topic. I was no longer keen on politics - which was part of the story in Deception Point - and I did not enjoy writing with a female lead. I had been far more interested in the Vatican, Langdon, codes, symbology, and art. I wasn't enjoying writing, I had no money, and I found myself wondering once again if I should give up. Fortunately, my wife has always been a tremendous support system and she encouraged me to keep at it.

77. In addition to Blythe's support, my parents (both avid readers) repeatedly assured me the novels were commercial and that I just needed to

find the right publisher. My lone advocate at Simon & Schuster seemed to be my editor, Jason Kaufman, with whom I had developed a friendship and level of trust. He too had become deeply frustrated with the lack of publisher support I was receiving at Simon & Schuster.

78. The day after I submitted the Deception Point manuscript Blythe and I travelled on a much needed vacation to Mexico. It was thereon the Yucatan Peninsula, exploring the ancient Mayan pyramids and archaeological ruins of Chichen-Itza and Tulum, that I was (at last) able to leave behind the high tech world of Deception Point. We were immersed in ancient ruins and lost cultures, and this intriguing history was tickling my imagination again. I began to muster the sense that I might be able to write another novel. At that point, I had no doubt who my hero would be - I would return to the world of Robert Langdon. This sequel would ultimately become The Da Vinci Code.

79. The Da Vinci Code tells the story of professor Robert Langdon's race to decipher clues left for him by murdered Louvre curator Jacques Sauniere. Many of Sauniere's clues involve wordplay and relate to Leonardo da Vinci. The novel is, at its core, a treasure hunt through Paris, London, and Edinburgh. The story is a blend of historical fact, legend, myth, and fiction.

80. The novel's themes include: the sacred feminine; goddess worship; the Holy Grail; symbology; paganism; the history of the Bible and its accuracy, including the lost Gnostic Gospels; Templar history; the suppression of information by the church; the genealogy of Jesus; religious zealotry; and nature's grand design as evidence for the existence of God.

81. Many of the themes mentioned above have been popular topics for centuries. One can find explorations of them in many languages, including the languages of art, literature, and music (specifically the songs of the Troubadours, the game of Tarot cards, and travelling storytellers).

82. Many of the aforementioned themes from The Da Vinci Code fall in a category I often call "secret history" - those parts of mankind's past that allegedly have been lost or have become muddied by time, historical revision, or subversion. Of course, it is impossible when looking at secret history to know how much is truth, and how much is myth or fanciful invention. This blend of fact and potential intrigues me and is one of the reasons I love Leonardo da Vinci. Some of the most dramatic hints to possible lost "secret history" can be found in the paintings of Leonardo da Vinci, which seem to overflow with mystifying symbolism, anomalies, and

codes. Art historians agree that Da Vinci's paintings contain hidden levels of meaning that go well beneath the surface of the paint. Of course, some "secret history" may be fact, some fiction. This idea, of course, excited me as a potential plot device.

83. The Da Vinci Code has taken a lot of this infom1ation and put it forward in a different genre - that of a work of fiction, a thriller.

Researching and writing The Da Vinci Code

84. As with all of my books, so much time has passed since I researched each of the novels that it is hard for me to be exact about what sources I used at which precise point in the research and writing of each of the novels. In the case of The Da Vinci Code, Blythe and I spent a year or so travelling and conducting research during the writing of The Da Vinci Code. On the way, we met with historians and other academics and extended our travels from the Vatican and France to England and Scotland in order to investigate the historical underpinnings of the novel.

85. In preparing this statement, what I have done is gone back to my research books and notes and thought long and hard about how these big ideas came to the surface. In doing so, I see that more notes have survived from The Da Vinci Code than from any of my previous novels. This is not surprising. I am not a pack rat; in fact, I'm the exact opposite. In the same way that I try to trim the fat from my writing, I am constantly trimming excess clutter from my life. I have discarded most of my life's memorabilia, including personal letters, grade school essays, early diaries, and even academic commendations. I trashed my first manuscript for Digital Fortress (which I now regret) and even disposed of most lyric notes and demo tapes from my years as a songwriter. This may sound surprising, but both Digital Fortress and my music career felt like creative failures (as did Angels & Demons and Deception Point), and big boxes of old notes felt like painful reminders of years spent for naught. Also, we have moved house four times since I began writing, and heavy boxes of old notes rank very high on my "to discard" list.

86. I believe another reason that I found more notes from The Da Vinci Code is that it has been the most research intensive of my novels to date. It was my fourth novel, and I was getting better at writing; in the same way a

musician chooses to perform harder and harder pieces as he masters his instrument, I was eager to tackle more complicated plotlines. My research books for The Da Vinci Code are heavily marked with margin notes, sticky notes, underlining, highlighting, inserted pieces of paper, etc. A good portion of these notes (as with Angels & Demons) are in my wife's handwriting. She is passionate about art and secret history and was enjoying educating herself and being involved in the research. For example, in Angels & Demons, she may have found me the exact specifications of Berriini's Fountain of the Four Rivers. With The Da Vinci Code, however, she was reading entire books, highlighting exciting ideas, and urging me to read the material myself and find ways to work the ideas in to the plot. In particular, she became passionate about the history of the Church's suppression of women, and she lobbied hard for me to make it a primary theme of the novel. Blythe also tends to save far more memorabilia than I do; many of the research notes were now hers, and more of them found their way into safe-keeping.

87. Looking back at the books, I can see that we were highlighting all the big concepts that eventually appeared in the final draft of the book. In the following paragraphs, I have noted specific parts of source works we looked at to illustrate this point - this is not an exhaustive review of the research we did, but it gives an indication of the parameters and extent of the research.

88. In beginning to write The Da Vinci Code, I tried to place my head back in to the world of Robert Langdon - the world of art, religion, secrets, and symbols. In exploring his world anew, I began mulling over much of the information that had been leftover from my Angels & Demons research. This included my research on the brotherhood of the Masons and on The Knights Templar. As I have pointed out, the links between the Illuminati and the Masons are well documented, and one can hardly read about the Masons and not also read about the Knights Templar.

89. Blythe and I began buying additional research books on these groups. We already owned several books about the Masons (e.g. Encyclopaedia of Freemasonry, Morals & Dogma). In looking back at what we were buying at around this time, the titles included: The Hiram Key, by Christopher Knight and Robert Lomas (D.44); The History of the Knights Templars, by Charles G. Addison (D.23); The Knights Templar and their Myth, by Peter Partner; and Born in Blood, by John J. Robinson (D.55). All four books are listed in the

partial bibliography I produced for the Synopsis for The Da Vinci Code, which I later submitted to publishers, including Random House (see 163).

90. From my research in Angels & Demons, I had read extensively on the Templars, including the legend of "The Money Pit" - buried Templar treasure in Nova Scotia. This well-documented legend (literally buried treasure) held my interest for a time, and I toyed with it as an element for this new novel. I soon decided that Nova Scotia was not an ideal setting for a novel because it did not afford me the many options I would need for dramatic settings. In addition, I longed to put Robert Langdon back in the world of Angels & Demons - and that meant Europe.

91. At the outset of the project, one of my desires was to explore the origin of the Bible. The Bible is, in many respects, like any other compilation - it is a heavily edited collection of many authors' works. Even so, many people accept what is said in the Bible to be absolute fact. Another reason for selecting the topic of the Bible was my fascination with religion in general. To put it at its simplest, although religion often did good things and helped a lot of people, I could see that there were also many situations where any religion could be used for evil purposes. I found this clash to be potentially fertile ground in which to plant the seeds of my novel. I thought that perhaps this would be the theme, or "big idea" of the novel.

92. The theme of the Bible and religion took me to the Gnostic Gospels (essentially those parts of the Bible that were drafted, but ultimately did not appear in the final version and, therefore had not been widely read). Since visiting Rome while researching Angels & Demons I remained fascinated by what could be buried in the Vatican secret archives - those miles and miles of books must contain something pretty interesting - what could it be? At this early stage I thought that the answer to this question would be, in essence, material contained in alternative drafts of the Bible and the Gnostic Gospels - the story we read in the Bible is a partial story and it is an edited story. Many historians believe that the Gnostic Gospels are one of the missing pieces.

The Hiram Key - Knight & Lomas (D.44)

93. Angels & Demons had given me the chance to build on my knowledge of Constantine and the history of Christianity. I thought that it may be an idea to look at that history through a slightly different lens, that

lens being the exploration of those books of the Bible that were omitted from Constantine's version. An important book for this early research was The Hiram Key by Christopher Knight and Robert Lomas. This book examines the role of the Masons and The Knights Templar in excavating and then hiding a cache of early Christian writings. It also mentions the family of Jesus (siblings as opposed to children), the origins of Christianity, the Gnostic Gospels, and Rosslyn Chapel, in Edinburgh.

94. Looking back at my copy of The Hiram Key. I can see that either Blythe or myself has underlined passages that speculate as to the nature of what the Templars found and the subsequent impact on Christianity. We also underlined sections that deal with Constantine and the importance of Sol Invictus in determining modern Christian dates and practices.

95. I can see from our copy of The Hiram Key (D.44) that there is a mix of handwriting (quite extensive in parts) and markings (pencil, pen and highlighter pens) made by Blythe and me. In my childhood, I was taught never to write in books. To this day, I still have a strong aversion to it. (In fact, when I first became published and people asked me to sign their editions, I felt funny about it.) For this reason, my margin notes often are very light or taken down on a separate piece of paper. Blythe does not share my idiosyncrasy, and she often marks books very heavily. She also often produced research documents for me as a result of her studies of the books. An example from The Hiram Key is "hiram's key notes" (D.332). It can be seen from that document that she included a number of page references which she thought I should consult.

96. The above references to my books and documents are byway of example (as are the other examples I cite in this statement). When I am researching and writing a novel I read a lot of material. There is, of course, additional material in all of these sources which I would have seen, either because I read the book or because the research would suggest I read certain sections. Usually, I carefully read the notes Blythe prepared for me, but on some occasions she prepared notes that were either too lengthy (which I skimmed or ignored), seemed off-topic (notes that were of interest to her, but for which I had no use), or were outdated (sometimes I asked for information and then changed my mind or deleted that plot point).

The Templar Revelation- Pichzett & Prince (D. 53)

97. One of the new research books we found that I found most intriguing was The Templar Revelation. I think we discovered this book by chance during one of my book signings for Deception Point at a large chain bookstore. On our copy, I see its cover includes the tagline "Secret Guardians of the True Identity of Christ". Even today, this kind of book is the type that we would pick up. The cover of our copy of Templar Revelation bears a symbol with which we were already acquainted --the ankh which is mentioned in Angels & Demons by symbologist Robert Langdon (Corgi, page 253). I think this discovery was very early on in the research process --at this stage, I did not yet have a title for the novel. I was still hunting around for the "big idea".

98. The Templar Revelation discussed secret Templar history and the possible involvement of Leonardo da Vinci. This Da Vinci connection fit well into my desire to write in Langdon's domain, the world of art. I became excited about using Leonardo da Vinci as an historical touchstone and plot device for my new novel. Bernini had been central to Angels & Demons and I had enjoyed writing that book. Moreover, I knew Blythe was an enormous fan of Leonardo da Vinci and would be eager to help me research. It was probably at about this time that I came up with the title The Da Vinci Code.

99. Leonardo da Vinci is often described as a man who awoke from a deep slumber only to find that the rest of the world was still sleeping. An artist, inventor, mathematician, alchemist, he was a man centuries ahead of his time. Perhaps the greatest scientist the world had ever seen, Da Vinci faced the challenge of being a modem man of reason born into an age of religious fervour; an era when science was synonymous with heresy. Men like Galileo and Copernicus, in studying astronomy and the heavens, were considered trespassers -invaders in a sacred domain whose mysteries previously had been reserved for the traditional scholars of heaven -the priests. The Church believed that the magic of the universe (the stars, the seasons; planets) were evidence of God's almighty design. They were miracles to be revered as such, not scientific riddles to be unravelled and de mystified with telescopes and mathematics.

100. Surprisingly, despite Da Vinci's lifelong conflict with religion, he was a deeply spiritual man. Like Galileo, Da Vinci looked at nature's miracles, and in them, he saw proof of a divine Creator. The ratio PHI is a

perfect example of this. Leonardo da Vinci employed this "Golden Ratio" in much of his f religious artwork. His philosophy was one in which science and religion lived in harmony. As I have said, I have a fascination with the interplay between science and religion, and I think that's one of the reasons I became so quickly engrossed in Leonardo da Vinci as a topic. He is perhaps the perfect subject for me, given my love of codes, science, religion, art and secrecy.

101. As I stated earlier, I studied art history at the University of Seville. The course covered the entire history of World Art, including, of course, Leonardo Da Vinci. The course made a great impression on me. I was only 21 years old at the time.. but years later, reading Templar Revelation (D.S3), I recalled the professor's observations about the dark quality of The Last Supper. I was starting to sense I had another Langdon novel in the works. Angels & Demons had touched on Bernini's secrets; and now I could see a path where I could do the same with Da Vinci.

102. Da Vinci is also the connection between art and the secret society that I chose to include in The Da Vinci Code - the Priory of Sion. Like Da Vinci's paintings, the Priory of Sion and Da Vinci's involvement with it is discussed in Templar Revelation (D..S3). I had included the subject of cults and secret societies in my previous novel, Angels & Demons, by referring to the Illuminati. Both Digital Fortress and Deception Point featured secretive organizations. With Langdon the common protagonist to both Angels & Demons and The Da Vinci Code, and having played around with the idea of the Masons being the secret society, I decided to include a reference to another cult in The Da Vinci Code, namely the Priory of Sion. I also made the decision to shelve the Masons for another day.

103. From the moment I started conceiving The Da Vinci Code, it was a certainty that art would feature significantly. Langdon is not merely a symbologist, he is an art historian. From looking back at my documents and sources, I can see that Blythe and I purchased many books with information about art and codes in art, Templar Revelation (D.S3) being one of them.

104. There is a note on the first page of our copy of Templar Revelation (D.53) referencing Poussin, the Last Supper, Teniers and Notre Dame. In the book, there is also an analysis of the painting Virgin of the Rocks. In my printed research, one of the documents is entitled "Interesting Leonardo stories" (D.334). This features some quotes from Templar Revelation and

analysis of Virgin of the Rocks. In another document "DVC -TO ADDI' (D.91!, there is information on Botticelli, the artist that features in Margaret Starbird's book The Woman with the Alabaster Jar{D.59) (a book which I mention again below).

105. Many other books were bought by Blythe, or were simply in our possession as art lovers, on Leonardo da Vinci. The partial bibliography on my website lists The Notebooks of Leonardo da Vinci, which I know we own but cannot find. It also lists, Prophecies, by Leonardo da Vinci; Leonardo da Vinci: Scientist, Inventor, Artist; and Leonardo da Vinci, the Artist and the Man. It is most likely that I read these texts online, found something useful, and therefore credited them. I particu1arly recall using Prophecies for a quote.

106. More information on coded paintings was found in book The Tomb of God, by Richard Andrews and Paul Schellenberger (D.24). For example, its front cover is the painting Les Bergers d' Arcadie II by Nicolas Poussin. On the title page there is a note in Blythe's handwriting. There is a chapter on Poussin and Teniers, with a note in Blythe's hand-writing "work Poussin into Mystery?".

107. Cocteau is another artist who features in The Da Vinci Code for his coded works, particularly with regard to Notre Dame. Looking back at my notes and research texts, it would appear that most of this information came from Templar Revelation (D.53). (I know that Holy Blood, Holy Grail also examines hidden meaning in Cocteau's work, but The Da Vinci Code and Holy Blood, Holy Grail discuss different pieces.)

108. I should mention that Blythe wrote similar notes in many of our research books, usually urging me to take note of some interesting fact she had found. She was becoming more and more intrigued by the information we were learning, and she wanted me to incorporate all of it (which I could not possibly do). She often playfully chided me about my resolve to keep the novel fast-paced (always at the expense of her research). In return, I jokingly reminded her that I was trying to write a thriller, not a history book. In the end, we found a comfortable balance of pace and history, and we had a wonderful time throwing ideas back and forth. Blythe's female perspective was particularly helpful with this book, which deals so heavily with concepts like the sacred feminine, goddess worship and the feminine aspect of spiritually.

109. Somewhere during the research for The Da Vinci Code (and well before I started writing anything), I learned that Mary Magdalene was not in fact a prostitute (as I had been taught in Sunday school) - this is alluded to in Templar elevation and The Woman with the Alabaster Jar. This stunned me I was amazed that this piece of mis-information had survived so long. I was curious about what other mis-information remained part of official church doctrine once again, I was motivated to dig deeper. So we purchased some of the books instead in Templar Revelation, including The Woman with the Alabaster jar, by Margaret Starbird. I can't remember how we found this book - perhaps by Blythe searching in the internet, or perhaps simply by seeing it mentioned in Templar Revelation. The Woman with the Alabaster Jar focuses on the story of the misrepresented Mary Magdalene. I am fairly sure that it was his book which led us to the second Margaret Starbird book, The Goddess the Gospels (0.58).

110. As I read more about the lost books of the Bible, I was reminded of the old truism that since the beginning of recorded time, history has been written by the "winners" (those societies and belief systems that conquered and survived). Despite an obvious bias in this accounting method, we still measure the "historical accuracy" of a given concept by examining how well it concurs with our existing historical record. I was becoming more open to considering different versions of history.

111. Although I was skeptical at first about Margaret Starbird's books, Blythe reacted to them with enormous passion and enthusiasm. In fact, I'm not sure I had ever seen Blythe as passionate about anything as she became for the historical figure of Mary Magdalene (particularly the idea that the church had unfairly maligned her). Blythe even bought a painting of Mary Magdalene and hung it over her desk. Margaret Starbird's books opened our eyes to the concept of the Church's subjugation of the sacred feminine. But I still needed some convincing. At about this time my wife ordered a series of three historical films by the film maker Donna Rea ~ (Women & Spirituality). I found the films absolutely fascinating. I was amazed to learn of the existence of a church publication called The Malleus Maleficarum (D.45), a book that counseled people how to identify and murder women who fit the church's broad definition of "witch". I began to realize that history barely mentioned the Church's systemic subjugation of the sacred feminine. The films also mentioned the Gnostic Gospels, pre-historic art honouring the

female as life giver, the symbol of the inverted triangle - the womb, Catholicism, symbols, the serpent being linked to religion, the obliteration of 25,000 years of goddess worship by the ancient Greeks (Athena, formerly a goddess of love becomes a war goddess and - strikingly - sprang from the head of Zeus, as Eve came from Adam's rib).

112. My eyes were now wide open to the idea of the suppression of the sacred feminine. My reading convinced me that there was a great case to be put forward that woman had been unfairly treated in the eyes of society for hundreds of years if not longer, and that religion had played a big part: in this. An example of where I worked this conception into The Da Vinci Code is on pages 173- 74 {Corgi).

113. However, my "big idea" had not yet fully formed itself. At this point, I might have toyed with writing a few sections of the book (in no particular order) to get a feel of the characters or setting, but I still wasn't entirely decided on the backbone of the story. It seemed to be evolving into something much more interesting than simply Da Vinci's paintings and the origins of the Bible. I could not imagine how this information about suppressing the sacred feminine had been done or why it was not known in the mainstream. Blythe, as well as helping e with the research, encouraged me to incorporate the theme of the sacred feminine and the goddess. From looking back at my documents and sources, I can see, for example, that on a note inserted into the inside cover of The Woman 's Dictionary of Symbols and Sacred Objects, by Walker (0..60), Blythe has written a note "goddess section" (0.238); and on page 202, she has written "read all" by the Goddess entry. Further, in a document entitled "DVC 16 - TO ADDI" (D.91); sections of material either Blythe provided or I toyed with include references to themes such as the sacred feminine, fairytales, lsis, and other topics which feature abundantly in the Margaret Starbird books.

114. Margaret Starbird's books were a big inspiration -the image she created of Mary Magdalene being the bride, the lost sacred feminine, was very elegant - it seemed like the "big idea" --like the core of a classic fairy tale or enduring legend. This concept of the lost sacred feminine became the backbone of The Da Vinci Code and would become the central theme of the novel --in the Acknowledgements I thank my wife and my mother and note that the novel "draws heavily on the sacred feminine". Also, the reason why Sauniere is so keen for Sophie to meet with Langdon is because of a shared

interest in goddess worship. In the book Langdon's yet to be published manuscript is called "Symbols of the Lost Sacred Feminine" (The Da Vinci Code, Corgi, pages 42 -143)

115. Indeed, at the very start of my Synopsis, for The Da Vinci Code (0.4), which I refer to below, I included the quote from Genesis "God created man in his own image male and female". I did this to reinforce the central theme of the book, which was there right from the start of the writing. In The Da Vinci Code, I also decided to describe the Priory as "the pagan goddess worship cult" (Corgi page 158) in order to further steer the emphasis of the novel towards Mary Magdalene and the lost feminine. This portrayal of the role and ideology of the Priory was my personal interpretation.

116. I also included a quotation attributed to Pope Leo X, which appears in The Hiram Key "It has served us well, this myth of Christ", because the book would feature the history of Christianity. My dad is a great sounding board, and I still remember talking to him about the idea of writing a novel about the lost sacred feminine. He seemed uncertain but noted (tongue in cheek) that if I wrote a book with the central theme of the sacred feminine, I may sell more books and able to pay my rent because most book-buyers were women.

Opus Dei

117. In The Da Vinci Code I also wanted to include the grey area in religion and did so by including Opus Dei. This grey area was also explored in Angels & Demons. Opus Dei is a very devout Catholic group, which like many fervent religious groups is met with suspicion and mistrust; only some of which is justified. While Opus Dei is a very positive force in the lives of many people, for others, affiliation with Opus Dei has been a profoundly negative experience. Their portrayal in the novel is based on books written about Opus Dei as well as my own personal interviews with current and former members. In both books I wanted to demonstrate that very few things are black and white; all bad or all good.

118. As an extension to the theme of a religious gray area, I also referred to corporal mortification -the practice of self flagellation. For most people, the practice sounds abhorrent. Yet, from my years living in Spain I saw that it is a big part of modem Catholicism in Spain. Every year on Easter prominent

bankers and lawyers put chains on their legs and march through the streets as their yearly penance. The practice itself is not uncommon.

The Bloodline

119. I reached a stage in my research where I had plenty of material for the next novel-- perhaps even too much. Blythe had been a great advocate for the novel focusing even more on the area of the suppression of the sacred feminine -he also lobbied hard for me to find a way to use a theory which concerned e legend of the Holy Grail --the so-called "bloodline theory". This is a well documented theory which, by this stage in the research process, we had read about in many books. for example, in The History of the Knights Templars" by Charles G. Addison (D.23), the Introduction (written in 1997 by David Hatcher Childress) says that "Different versions of the legend exist with the two mo t prominent stating that the Holy Grail is the cup or chalice used by Christ at the Last Supper or, alternatively, the genetic blood-lineage of Jesus." The "bloodline theory" is what Hatcher Childress describes as "the genetic blood-lineage of Jesus'

120. Initially, I was reluctant to include the bloodline theory at all, finding it too incredible and inaccessible to readers - I thought it was a step too far. However, it after much discussion arid brainstorming with Blythe, I eventually became convinced that I could introduce the idea successfully. Blythe had suggested introduce it as a part of the Goddess worship theme - the lost sacred feminine being embodied by the Church of Magdalene that never was. The more I read on this topic - both in Blythe's notes and independently in the books and on the internet - the more plausible I found the storyline.

121. I am positive that Blythe and I read about the bloodline theory in many sources before reading any of Holy Blood, Holy Grail. From looking back at my source, all of which I am sure I looked at while researching The Da Vinci Code, I have found numerous references in other texts and materials to the theory.

122. The theory appears in all of the following books: The History of the Knights Templars, by Charles G. AddjsoniD.23); Templar Revelation, by Picknett & Prince (D.5); The Goddess In the Gospels, by Margaret Starbird (0.58); The Woman with the Alabaster Jar, by Margaret Starbird (D. 59); and

The Tomb of God, by Andrews & Schellenberger (D.24). It also is noted in my research documents, for example, documents entitled "Holy Grail Info" called "grail%2fjeusbloodline info" (D.330); "Myths and Stories of the Knights Templar" (.235); and "MASONS" (D.261).

123. In preparing this statement, I have also looked at my Synopsis for The Da Vinci Code (D4) (I refer to this document in more detail in 161 below), which I wrote in January 2001 long before we bought or consulted Holy Blood, Holy Grail. This has helped me to work out what were the main sources for he bloodline point. In the Synopsis, I refer to the fact that Merovingian comes from "MER = sea and VIGNE == vine" (which is referenced The Woman with the Alabaster Jar, page 62). Furthermore, when Langdon is explaining the bloodline theory to Sophie on the Seine, I included a note to readers: "including countless biblical references to Jesus as 'bridegroom" Mary Magdalene as the bride and the vine bearing his sacred fruit, and dozens of Vatican-banned gospels...." This material is all dealt with comprehensively in Margaret Starbird's books. The first three chapters of The Woman with the Alabaster Jar are called: The Lost Bride, The Bridegroom, and The Blood Royal and the Vine.

124. I am certain that I read the above books and documents before I looked at Holy Blood, Holy Grail. All of my early research came from other sources, which included those listed above and many related websites and articles. (I describe below how I eventually used Holy Blood, Holy Grail).

Secrets, treasure hunts, symbology. codes

125. As with m earlier books, there is a lot in The Da Vinci Code that is familiar - a murder, a chase through foreign locations, the action taking place all in 24 hours, a code a ticking clock, strong male and female characters, and a love interest. The book also builds on what I saw as the great leaps forward I made in Angels & Demons. Again, it is thriller as academic lecture, there is plenty of hidden formation, symbology, codes and treasure hunts. And even more so than in Angels & Demons, the reader is accelerated through the book - I used short chapters, ideally with some form of cliff-hanger at the end of each one.

126. In the following paragraphs I have highlighted some of the many other things that appear The Da Vinci Code - they are all important, and I

think they are all reasons why the book has had the impact that it has. The list, however, is not exhaustive - for that, the book itself should be consulted.

127. In The Da Vinci Code, Sophie Neveu witnesses Sauniere taking part in a Hieros Gamos ritual; an event that is to set the background of her relationship with her grandfather, and also combine the bloodline theory with that of Goddess worship. Starbird's books in particular view the bloodline theory from a Lost Sacred Feminine perspective. While the history of Hieros Gamos is well documented, I made up the idea that it was practiced by the Priory. The description of the ritual itself was inspired by Stanley Kubrick's film 'Eyes Wide Shut'.

128. In my synopsis (described below) I tell readers to imagine this movie, which is probably because I had recently written a synopsis for Angels &; Demons that was geared to film producers (in an attempt to sell the movie rights), and conjuring that image seemed an effective way to convey the mystery and scope of what I was imagining. The images of the clothing I describe came from Blythe, who found them on numerous magical or ritualistic websites, quite apart from anything Priory related. The white and black of the male and female costumes were described on these websites. I recall being pleased that this dove-tailed so nicely with the white and black Cryptex I had planned.

129. The first place I look for ideas on symbols is The Dictionary of Symbols, by Chevalier (D.30). This enormous tome is essentially a dictionary that tells us the origins of symbols that we see every day. Looking at my copy I can see that Blythe has written a note in the inside cover saying "pentagram - the key to higher knowledge and opened door to what was secret". She has also written: chalice, womb, Vulva - MM as vessel". These are all symbols that appear in The Da Vinci Code. Another symbology text I used a lot in writing The Da Vinci Code is The Woman's Dictionary of Symbols and Sacred Objects(Q,,60), mentioned above. I feel that one of the most effective ways of putting forward a theory, is demonstrating the symbology substantiated in it. Suggesting the "chalice" of the Holy Grail is Mary Magdalene's womb is far more convincing if one understands the symbology behind the image of a chalice.

130. Another significant symbol which I wanted to include is the mathematical symbol PH , the Divine Proportion. As with other symbols in The Da Vinci Code, PHI ties nature to religion, the divine feminine and art. It

also links directly with the pentagram and hence Da Vinci's Vitruvian Man. I know about PHI from my father, from my early studies in art and architecture (although my art teachers called it "The Golden Ratio"), as well as from books such as Huntley's The Divine Proportion (D.40)

131. While on the subject of symbology, in one of my documents, "DYC - TO ADDI" (1.91) is a passage I contemplated including about the Fleur de Lis: a significant symbol in The Da Vinci Code.

132. As I state above codes are very much a relic from my childhood and have always fascinated me. For the same reasons that I made Vittoria Vetra an entanglement physicist in Angels & Demons and Robert Langdon a symbologist, I made Sophie Neveu a cryptologist. In Angels & Demons I was particularly keen on the idea of using codes, but did not have as much occasion for it - in that book, I made more use of poems and riddles. In The Da Vinci Code, I decided to explore the device further. As a result, codes feature most prominently in The Da Vinci Code and it therefore seemed appropriate to have Sophie as an 'expert' or teacher in order to help solve them; just as Vittoria explained the scientific concepts in Angels & Demons. As a plot device, it also linked her to Langdon. In addition, Sophie's relationship with Sauniere - solving codes and embarking on treasure hunts - is reminiscent of my own with my father. I wanted to portray this relationship in the novel.

133. I believe another reason I decided to make Sophie a cryptologist is that I recalled how much fun I'd had writing the "cryptologist heroine" (Susan Fletcher) in my first novel Digital Fortress. Back then, there was a naive joy about the writing process (before the frustrations of the publishing business set in), and I think part of me wanted to revisit that by using my new-found plotting skills to reinvent my original character archetype and really put her through her paces. .

134. Poems and anagrams were again two forms of codes or riddles that featured prominently in my childhood. As I have already mentioned, my father used poems in annual Christmas treasure hunts to lead us to our "hidden treasure'. I found among my Da Vinci Code research my father's Christmas Treasure hunt from 1982, Chapter 23 of The Da Vinci Code was directly inspired by one of my childhood treasure hunts.

135. An important code in The Da Vinci Code is the Fibonacci sequence, my knowledge of which came from books such as The Divine Proportion by

H. E. Huntley (40), and my father. Not only did I think Fibonacci was an interesting code which fit in comfortably with symbols such as PHI, but it was a plot device used to introduce Sophie to Langdon. I found among my Da Vinci Code research a document entitled "Leonardo da Vinci and the Fibonacc lequence" (0.183) [sic], which is a series of specific questions I prepared for Blythe to research on things such as Fibonacci and the Vitruvian Man. PHI, Fibonacci, the Vitruvian Man and Da Vinci all complement each other; they can be linked to so many of the same themes.

136. When I was writing Digital Fortress I researched cryptology and came across Caesar boxes, invented by Julius Caesar. I was also familiar with the notebooks of Leonardo da Vinci, who created many ingenious machines most of which were never made. At some point I had seen a blueprint of portable safe. It was my idea that Sauniere and Sophie call it a Cryptex. It was used as a dramatic device to release information slowly. It is essentially a Da Vinci invention with the vinegar and the papyrus. However, it was never made, and I did elaborate a bit on the design. The black and white of the Cryptex were used to symbolize the masculine and feminine theme that runs throughout the novel.

137. The Atbash Cypher is an ancient substitution code based on the Hebrew alphabet. I used it in The Da Vinci Code as the code required to open the Cryptex. The keyword was "Baphomet", a headstone worshipped by the Templars as a pagan fertility god, traditionally represented as a ram or goat's head. Application of the Atbash Cypher to the word "Baphomet", results in the word Sophia - the ancient Greek word for wisdom. I was really amazed by how this code worked, particularly as Baphomet ties in so well with themes of the Templars and sex rites. I acquired information on the Atbash Cypher, Baphomet and Sophia from Templar Revelation and Tomb of God. On page 399 of my copy of Tomb of God(D .24), Blythe has written the notes "Sophia/wisdom, Baphomet/Sophia" and "very cool. Also see TR". It is dealt with on p.109 Templar Revelation (D.53), which Blythe has also underlined. During the preparation of this statement, I have been told that Holy Blood, Holy Grail also mentions Baphomet in the context of Templar worship - the Templars were accused of worshipping fake gods. However, in Holy Blood, Holy Grail, Baphomet is suggested to be a "bearded male head".

138. In The Da Vinci Code another device I used to maintain suspense was the mysterious "keystone" that the characters are searching for - a

rosewood box, containing the Priory's greatest secret. "Keystone" is an architectural term used to denote the central stone in an archway, supporting the archway and preventing it from collapsing. Its significance in The Da Vinci Code was entirely my creation, and has no bearing on the actual meaning of the word. It was my idea to link it with the Priory and the bloodline, and it was also my idea that the Grand Master and his seneschals would keep the Priory secret to the exclusion of all others. I decided that the keystone would be the means of keeping the secret. In The Da Vinci Code it is called a clef de voute, because Sauniere is French. It is far more plausible that the Priory would use the French nomenclature.

Locations

139. Locations are very significant to me when writing. In both Angels & Demons and The Da Vinci Code, the locations are often as important as the art itself in telling the story and solving the codes. In my Synopsis for The Da Vinci Code, instead having numbered chapters, I used location headings. Locations not only make the read more enjoyable (in my opinion), they add to the credibility of the ideas put forward. They also give the character of Robert Langdon a further opportunity to "teach" readers. Most people are unaware of the pagan origins of the Pantheon, for example, or the existence of demons' holes in some churches.

140. In The Da Vinci Code, I wanted to pay homage to the Louvre; a work of art itself. In the novel it is the final resting place for the Holy Grail. I spent time researching I. M. Pei, the architect of the famous and controversial Pyramid. I do not actually own any books, about or by Pei, and I recall doing most of the research online at an architectural website (I believe the site was www.greatbuildings.com, which I see is still active today and still offers the I. M. Pei renderings). This enabled me to download CAD renderings of famous buildings, including the Louvre Pyramid. I remember this because I became very frustrated that my inexpensive computer was too weak to fully display these spatial models without crashing. Nonetheless, I could scroll through the rendered frames slowly, and I became very excited about the Internet as a tool for researching the architecture of the buildings that I would be writing about (Notre Dame, the Louvre, Westminster Abbey, etc). In addition, I found among my research a document that refers to various

other sources - presumably from the internet, entitled "Pyramid. The Mona Lisa. Louvre Info. Mitterrand" (D. 192).

141. Other sites that feature or are mentioned in the book, for example St. Sulpice, Notre Dame and Westminster Abbey, I either visited myself, researched on the internet or used guide books. One useful research source was Fodor's Guide to Paris 2001 (D.35), which particularly has information on the Louvre, St. Sulpice, and Notre Dame.

142. A location that kept resurfacing during my research was that of Rosslyn Chapel in Scotland, famous for its symbology and links to the Templars. Rosslyn is one of the last locations visited in The Da Vinci Code, where Sophie finds her grandmother and brother, and her history and heritage are revealed. The predominant source for my Rosslyn information was The Hiram Key, a lot of which is devoted to Rosslyn. Looking back at my copy, Blythe has made copious notes inside on Rosslyn. She also compiled two research documents called "Rosslyn Castle Info (plus notes at end on RBS and HK)" (D.181) and "Rosslyn highlights" (D.349), much of which appears to come from The Hiram Key. I also took information from the Rosslyn Chapel website (www.rosslynchapel.org,uk).

143. In The Da Vinci Code, Rosslyn is just another location, whereas in other texts, including Holy Blood, Holy Grail, it is suggested that Rosslyn is the final resting place for the Grail. It seemed more appropriate to me that Mary Magdalene would be returned by the Priory to France. The symbolism of the inverted angle at Louvre - a chalice - appealed to me, so I returned to focus to the Louvre, where the thriller began.

Review of research sources for The Da Vinci Code

144. A lot has happened since I researched this book, and I cannot remember every detail about which sources I used for what aspects of the novel. In general, however, the history and theory in The Da Vinci Code was readily available in texts other than Holy Blood, Holy Grail at the time I wrote the book. Moreover, Blythe and I studied these texts prior to seeing Holy Blood, Holy Grail.

145. I did look at Holy Blood, Holy Grail (D.25) before completing the book (and in the text I refer to it as being "perhaps the best known tome" on the topic of the bloodline theory (The Da Vinci Code, Corgi, page 339-340)).

But the fact remains that my sources for the ideas which I am alleged to have copied from Holy Blood, Holy Grail did not include Holy Blood, Holy Grail.

146. When I did finally look at a copy of Holy Blood, Holy Grail I was surprised by what I read on the cover. This surprise found its way into the pages of The Da Vinci Code. Characters in my novels often speak for me, or reflect my experiences (for example, I have mentioned Sophie and her childhood treasure hunts). In Da Vinci Code, Sophie first sees a book called Holy Blood, Holy Grail in Sir Leigh Teabing's study -she notes that the cover is emblazoned with the words: INTERNATIONAL BESTSELLER. Sophie is puzzled and comments, "An international bestseller? I've never heard of it." (Corgi, page 340). Sophie's words echo my own personal surprise when I finally saw the cover of Holy Blood, Holy Grail and realized it was an international bestseller. I'd never heard of it until I'd seen it mentioned in some of our other research books.

147. I chose to include the title of Holy Blood, Holy Grail in this chapter (along with three other non-fiction books - The Templar Revelation (D.53), The Woman with the Alabaster Jar (D. 59), and The Goddess in the Gospels (D.58) in the hope that any readers who became curious about the some of the ideas in my book, a fictional thriller, would know where to turn to find jump-off points for additional reading material and more details. Maybe it's because I have been a teacher, but I have always enjoyed suggesting books to people, especially on esoteric topics. Offering the reader a glance at someone else's bookshelf seemed like an entertaining way to offer other reading material. I did the exact same thing in Angels & Demons, in which I described a bookshelf bearing three books (The God Particle (D.47), The Tao of Physics, and God: the Evidence (D.37). In that case, my hope was that readers who wanted to know more about the subject matter of that book would know where to look for additional reading material.

148. Holy Blood, Holy Grail maybe a well known source, but it is not one I consulted until the storyline of my book was very well developed. I found most of the relevant ideas in my Templar and Masonic books (such as The History of the Knights Templar (D.23), The Knights Templar and their Myth, Born in Blood (D.55), and The Hiram Key (D.44)); The Templar Revelation; Margaret Starbird's books - Woman with the Alabaster Jar (D.59) and Goddess in the Gospels {D.S8).

149. I also looked at Donna Read's programs, Women & Spirituality, and my books on codes and symbols (Dictionary of Symbology, by Chevalier (0.30), Codes, Ciphers and other Cryptic and Clandestine Communication, by Wrixon (0.61), The Divine Proportion, by Huntiey (0.40), Dictionary of Symbols, by Liungman (D.48), The Woman's Dictionary of Symbols and Sacred Objects, by Walker D.60).and for some basic information about gargoyles, Fodor's Guide to Paris, 2001 (D.36)). I also looked at The Malleus Maleficarum, by Kramer and Sprenger (D.45), The Gnostic Gospels, by Elaine Pagels (D.51) (I had already read one of her books --The Origins of Satan (D.52), while researching Angels & Demons), and The Tomb of God, by Andrews & Schellenberger (D.24). To a lesser extent I relied on and got ideas from other books and materials, such as Joseph Campbell's book Transformations of Myth Through Time (D.29), and a TV show I saw of him being interviewed called "Power of Myth"; and Rule by Secrecy, by Marrs .(D.50) (this last book I read late in the writing of the novel).

150. Also, I made full use of the internet and what it offers. In the research and writing of The Da Vinci Code I looked at numerous online sources. I find the internet a great source of factual information, if used carefully. For example, if I needed to find a restaurant in Zurich for a particular scene, I would be able to find out the address and even what's on the menu by conducting as search online. This all adds detail to the descriptive parts of a novel that makes it all the more credible or realistic to the reader. I try to get these details right (even though do not always achieve this).

151. I often use the internet to give me a sense of whether or not an idea has potential. For example, if I hear a fact that sounds interesting and yet suspect, I will run a narrow search for that information and determine the credibility of people who have written about it. Invariably a narrow search will pull up specific passages from online excerpts of other books (promotional excerpts, commentary, reviews, Amazon, articles, etc.).

152. Large portions of the supporting research for The Da Vinci Code was performed online because of the ease of searching large numbers of documents or specific data and references. For example, with respect to information on I. M. Pei, while I do not actually own any books about or by M. Pei, I was able to find the relevant information online on architectural websites, online excerpts of books about Pei and other websites.

153. In addition I was helped in my research not only by Blythe but by Stan Planton, a librarian based at the University of Ohio. Stan had access to an incredible amount of online material and did "key-word searches" for me via his access to Lexis-Nexis. He sent me literally hundreds of texts from newspapers, journals, magazines, and other articles (including many European sources). In the preparation of this statement, I contacted Stan and spoke to him by telephone. He told me that he recalls doing keyword searches for -- (in his words) "Merovingian", "Magdalene", "Priory of Sion", "Templar"', "Grail", "Opus Dei" "bloodline of Christ" and many more. I asked him if he had copies of our correspondence. He looked for them but said that he had sent these emails to me more than three years ago and that they had been long since deleted. It is possible that some of the documents I have made available in the litigation include research papers that Stan found. I have searched my own computer files for electronic copies of Stan's research, but have found no such records. I believe that those records were stored on my old computer, which was damaged following a serious flood in about March 2004 when I also lost many of my documents and other materials. Two emails of the type of research that Stan said he completed for me are attached as Exhibit DB1.

154. In the late stages of writing The Da Vinci Code, Blythe and I started to use email more frequently to share ideas with each other. The reason for this is that more of our research was taking place on the Internet, and email became the most efficient way of sharing information. For Blythe, sending me cut-and-paste text or a clickable link to a large website was easier than printing out dozens of pages in hardcopy. This was especially true for websites that had lots of photographs (photos were very helpful in writing my descriptive passages, but they printed poorly and ate up expensive printer toner; I preferred to see them online). For some topics, Blythe pulled together many points and typed up a research document, usually covering the research that I had asked her to do on a particular topic. This new tool of email now meant that those research notes appeared in all kinds of different forms - her own extracts, clips from the internet, scans from source books, and website resource files. Sometimes I got a paper copy of those notes, usually an emailed copy, and sometimes both.

155. I don't like reading things on screen - my eye, sight is pretty good, but I find it tiring to look at the screen when reading. So, if I am at a point

where I want to introduce a nugget of information on a work of art, or of a tube station, or of an airfield n Kent, I usually print out the page from the Internet, or from Blythe's notes and move away from my desk and computer, sit down and read the material. I may highlight points with a pen, or I may move back to the screen to insert some bullet points. Sometimes I can become rather frustrated when presented with too much information. If Blythe's research is voluminous, I will sometimes read Blythe's note and ask her to produce something more concise and focused so that I have the very essence of the points.

156. I add Blythe's research to my own, and then I attempt to distil and make palatable to the reader the raw subject matter. I estimate that I weed out the vast proportion of the research, and present only what I regard as the most interesting bits for the reader. This painstaking process of researching and writing a novel has been described by me as a lot like making maple sugar candy. You have to tap hundreds of trees ...boil vats and vats of raw sap... evaporate the water ...and keep boiling until you've distilled a tiny nugget that encapsulates the essence. Of course, this requires liberal use of the delete key.

157. In many ways, editing yourself is the most important part of being a novelist - carving away superfluous text until your story stands crystal clear before your reader. For every page in each of my novels, I probably wrote ten that ended up in the trash. All of this work leads to the production of a manuscript, revised drafts, and then finally the finished novel. My tendency toward heavy editing ("trimming the fat" as I called it) fuelled the ongoing push-and-pull between Blythe and me. Blythe constantly urged me to add more facts and more history. I was always slashing out long descriptive passages in an effort to keep the pace moving. I remember Blythe once gave me an enormous set of architectural / historical notes for a short flashback I was writing about Notre Dame Cathedral. When I had finished the section, she was frustrated by how little of work actually made the final cut. In these situations, I always remind Blythe I was trying to write a fast-moving page-turner.

Writing The Da Vinci Code

158. My editor Jason Kaufman, has helped me piece together the dates of various events, from the point that I started writing in earnest, through to my move to Doubleday and the launch of The Da Vinci Code. He prepared for me a timeline, and the dates below are taken from that timeline.

159. In January 2001, I had submitted the Deception Point manuscript to Jason and was in Florida visiting my parents. I remember I was swimming in my parents' pool when Jason called. He told me that Pocket Books loved my Deception Point manuscript and wanted to sign me up for two more books. Jason told me he would call my literary agent and make the offer. I remember asking Jason not to call my agent quite yet. I had been thinking about my agenting situation for some time now, and I had a decision to make. My original literary agent George Wieser had passed away shortly after Digital Fortress had been published. By this point in my career, I had learned enough about publishing to know that if I were ever going to be a successful novelist, I would need team who could orchestrate a large-scale release of my novels.

160. I had been t inking of getting a new agent for some time now, and I had begun to make some inquiries. One agent's name - Heide Lange - had come up several times through various sources. Only a day or so after I had spoken to Jason, I remember reading online that Heide Lange recently had signed a new thriller writ Brad Thor to a million dollar publishing deal with Pocket Books. I was stunned. I wondered if Heide could get the same kind of money for my new thriller idea. As I researched Heide more carefully, I became very hopeful. On her website I noticed that she had agented several non-fiction books about art (including the classic bestseller "Drawing On The Right Side Of The Brain") as well as books on feminism, (including the famous international bestseller The G Spot, as well as The Feminist Memoir Project.) I recall becoming excited about Heide as a prospect. My new novel - -The Da Vinci Code -- was all about art and the sacred feminine. Who better to sell it than a woman who had already sold books on these same themes? Then I realized Heide's last name -- LANGE -- was an anagram of ANGEL. I am not superstitious, but I recall thinking this was a very good omen.

161. I got Heide's number off the Internet and phoned her office. I remember leaving her a voice mail that I hoped would persuade her to call me back. Rather than telling her I wanted her to be my agent, I shared with

her that Jason Kaufman at Pocket Books wanted to offer me a multiple book publishing deal, and that I needed someone to negotiate the contract. I figured that even a busy agent would jump at the chance to make 15% on a book deal without having to shop the manuscript. Sure enough, Heide called back within a few hours. I was impressed right from the start. In that short time span, Heide had already researched me online and sent her assistant out to buy one of my novels -- Digital Fortress. In fact, Heide had already read a few chapters when she called. I was captivated by Heide's enthusiasm, energy, and motivation. I immediately told Heide not to read Digital Fortress but rather to read Angels & Demons. I told her that the character and settings in Angels & Demons was "what I was all about"-- in particular the art and religious overtones. So Heide bought Angels & Demons, read it and loved it (as did her husband, John Chaffee). She signed me as a client immediately, and I had a good feeling that my career was at last going to turn the corner.

162. Heide and I were negotiating with Pocket, a division of Simon & Schuster that had an option on my next novel. As a part of that process, she suggested that I prepare several proposals to put forward in the hope of getting a multiple book deal. In early January 200l, I prepared short proposals for the novel ideas.

163. Heide asked me to expand upon the short outline I had drafted for The Da Vinci Code before submitting it to Pocket, in the hope that with a longer proposal I could get a better deal. I remember being very eager to impress Heide as much as she had impressed me, and so I plunged into writing this new synopsis with lots of energy. Unfortunately, because I was visiting my parents, I had no office space, and the only private place in their house was a tiny laundry room. I remember writing the expanded outline for The Da Vinci Code inside this tiny laundry room, sitting on a lawn-chair that had been set up at a makeshift desk made out of an ironing board. It was in this laundry room that I wrote an extensive 56 page outline, or Synopsis, for The Da Vinci Code (D.4). I remember trying hard to make the Synopsis exciting and cinematic. I had already written a similar synopsis of Angels & Demons in hopes of selling the novel to Hollywood, but that had never happened. When I finished The Da Vinci Code Synopsis, I sent it to Heide later in January 2001. This was considerably before the Da Vinci Code was actually written.

164. My Synopsis of the entire novel includes an initial bibliography for The Da Vinci Code. The initial, or 'partial', bibliography lists the books I used to lay out the rough story line. In this bibliography, Holy Blood, Holy Grail does not appear. That is because when I wrote the Synopsis I did not own a copy of Holy Blood, Holy Grail nor had I, or Blythe, read it. The partial bibliography is limited to 7 books:

The Templar Revelation - Picknett & Prince (D.53)
1. The Goddess in the Gospels - Starbird (D.58)
2. The Woman with the Alabaster Jar - Starbird (D.59)
3. The History of the Knights Templars - Addison (D.23)
4. The Hiram Key - Knight & Lomas (D.44)
5. The Knights Templar - Partner
6. Born in Blood - Robinson (D.55)

165. I have my copies of all of these books, save for The Knights Templar, by Peter Partner which I can't find. We have moved house three times since The Da Vinci Code research began -- and perhaps that book was lost during one of the moves. It is possible we loaned it out or misplaced it travelling. Also, it is possible that the Partner book was damaged and disposed of at the time of the flood.

166. The bibliography is "partial" in the sense that much of the research for the novel came from conversations, research trips, online sources and essentially sources that are hard to cite. I prepared a similar "partial" bibliography for Angels & Demons. This is not an unusual practice in circumstances where it is impossible to be absolutely specific about sources used; as is particularly the case where the internet is concerned and quoted authors are often not referenced.

167. The absence of Holy Blood, Holy Grail in my Synopsis' "partial" bibliography is in line with my clear recollection of referring to it only at a later time - it was not a crucial or important text in the creation of the framework of The Da Vinci Code.

168. Despite being certain that Holy Blood, Holy Grail (D.25), was not consulted until long after this outline was written and submitted, I have carefully gone through every point of this outline to ensure that there is nothing in here which suggests that, contrary to my recollection, I had seen Holy Blood, Holy Grail. Certainly no information or themes present in the outline are to be found only in Holy Blood, Holy Grail.

169. In the Synopsis, the murder in the opening scene features a ritualistic Masonic murder, based on that of Grand Master Hiram Abif. This points to The Hiram Key (D.44), which features Abif in its opening chapters. Also, the presence of elements such as the 'shroud", Sophia and Atbash in my Synopsis points very persuasively to Templar Revelation (which pays much attention to such topics) being an important source. By contrast, I have been told during the course of this litigation that Holy Blood, Holy Grail, barely mentions the shroud or Hiram Abif, and does not mention Atbash and Sophia. These sort of points illustrate to me that I was using The Hiram Key (D.44) and The Templar Revelation (D.53) as sources at the time (as well as the others in my partial bibliography) and indicate to me that I am correct in my recollection that I did not look at Holy Blood, Holy Grail until much later.

170. In February 2001, my editor, Jason Kaufman, moved to Doubleday, a division of Random House, Inc. He has told me that he showed my 56 page Synopsis to his boss, Bill Thomas, who loved it. Heide and I, however, were still negotiating with Pocket, who had an option on my next novel. Once the option period was complete, Doubleday made me an offer, slightly lower than that of Pocket, but I decided to accept it. The reasons for this were twofold: firstly, I wanted to continue working with Jason, in whom I have great faith; secondly, I had been so disappointed by Pocket's promotion of Angels & Demons and Deception Point, I felt I would have better luck starting afresh with a new publisher. I moved to Doubleday in mid-May 2001.

171. Between May 2001 and March 2002, I launched myself completely into the writing of The Da Vinci Code. During this period, Jason was not shown anything and I had very little contact with him or Heide. On March, 15, 2002, I sent Jason a draft of the first 190 pages of The Da Vinci Code, so that he could distribute it in advance of Doubleday's in-house pre-launch meeting for books published in Spring 2003. Jason then edited the draft and, after talking to me, distributed it on March 21, 2002.

172. A notable difference between the Synopsis and the final draft I submitted was the murder in the opening scene. In the final version of The Da Vinci Code I used the Vitruvian Man as a model for the opening murder scene (placing a dead character on the Louvre floor in the same body position as Leonardo da Vinci's the Vitruvian Man.) This idea was in my

mind very early as the Vitruvian man has always been a favourite of mine; I even have personal stationery featuring it. The Synopsis, as I have said, features a ritualistic Masonic murder, based on that of Grand Master Hiram Abif, featured at the beginning of The Hiram Key (D.44). The murder is still set in the Louvre, but I was having problems making this work, and I thought the Vitruvian man would be a far better murder victim.

173. Some of the action scenes are also different. For example, in the Synopsis I have Langdon and Sophie escape the assassin by jumping onto one of the Bateaux Mouches, on the Seine. It is here that Langdon reveals to Sophie the bloodline theory.

174. Another difference if that the peripheral characters are not as developed in the Synopsis; many are un-named or have different names. The Albino monk Silas, is a "massive Spaniard assassin" called Oedipus (an anagram of Opus Dei), Fache is the Capitaine of French Securite. In the final version the character of the Consul General does not exist, instead I included the Teabing character for reasons explained below. Aringarossa (spelt Arangirossa in the Synopsis - perhaps a typo) also plays a different role that is omitted from the final version of the novel.

Chapters 37, 55, and 58

175. By the time we obtained a copy of Holy Blood, Holy Grail (0.25), I had already written the Synopsis and the opening of the novel and had in place the themes of the sacred feminine, the bloodline, and secret history.

176. One of my favourite ways in which to share information with a reader is to have Langdon give an "academic lecture" on the topic. Writing one of his academic lectures is always a lot of fun but requires a firm grasp of specifics. Invariably, when I am preparing to write one of these academic lectures, I ask Blythe to collect and compile as much information as possible on the lecture topic. The Da Vinci Code includes lots of lectures - some long, some short -on topics such as Opus Dei (page 50 and see D.96, D.97, D.178 D.383, D.385 and D.387), the Mona Lisa (chapter 26, and see D.188, D.192 and D.338), goddess worship and suppression of the feminine (chapters 28 and 56, and D.174 and D.186), symbology (chapter 56), PHI (page 131), Fibonacci (page 92 and see D.180, D.183 and D.37), hidden meanings in paintings and

other art (chapters 58 and 61, and D.189 and D.191), and Rosslyn (chapter 104, and 0.181 andD.349)

177. There are three "academic lecture" chapters of The Da Vinci Code which contain information that is also in Holy Blood, Holy Grail (D.25). Those are chapter 37, which deals with the Templars, the Priory and the Grail, chapter 55, which deals with Christianity, Constantine and the Bible, and chapters 58, which deals with lost history, Jesus' marriage and the Grail as bloodline.

178. In each case, we turned to a number of books we now owned on the topics, including The Hiram Key (D.44), The Templar Revelation (D. 53), the Margaret Starbird books (D.58 & D,59), Holy Blood, Holy Grail (D.25), which --as I have explained above --was suggested reading in The Templar Revelation, and many others and which, by now, we had bought.

Chapter 55 -the origins of Christianity, Constantine, and the Bible lecture

179. Chapter 55 features Langdon revealing to Sophie his ideas about the origins of Christianity, Constantine and the Bible. These ideas also appeared in the Synopsis, and I re-wrote them for the final version of The Da Vinci Code. I was already familiar with much of this information, particularly that about Constantine, the Council of Nicea, and the surrounding politics. In general terms I have been aware of Constantine's role in the origin of the Bible as we know it for many years. In addition, I researched the topic while preparing the content of Angels & Demons. But I read a lot more about the topic while writing The Da Vinci Code.

180. On reviewing my research materials, it is clear to me that in the context of researching this particular "lecture", I also looked at The Hiram Key (D.44), The Templar Revelation (D.53), Holy Blood, Holy Grail (D.25), The Gnostic Gospels (D.51), and he Woman with the Alabaster Jar (D.59).

181. In the preparation of his statement, I have been shown a document entitled "Constantine". This as produced for me by Blythe (D.177 and D.322). It is obvious to me that the Constantine document is not in her words, but has been taken from other sources. It is not unusual for her to do this when we are working together. I will tell her the outline of a section of a book I have written and then ask her to go away and make a note of more specific

information about the topic which I can use to elaborate my text. At this stage both of us will have read a good deal about the topic, but she is better than me at producing a good summary of the material which we have looked at. If she finds a particular source which has many of the relevant facts collected together, she will make her note from that source. Sometimes she combines a number of sources in her notes to me. Sometimes she adds notes to me to look at other sources as well. There is no fixed pattern.

182. Returning to the "Constantine" document, I can tell from the style that it was not written by Blythe. Again, it was not at all uncommon for Blythe to send me text that was not her own (often she would transcribe paragraphs verbatim from sources in an effort to provide me the exact data I had requested). It has been pointed out to me that much of this particular Constantine document came from Holy Blood, Holy Grail. I would have known at the time that this was a summary of research she had prepared for me.

183. I would usually take a document like this, read it, consider it, and blend it in my mind with all the other material that I had read on the topic, I would cross reference or look again at other notes or other source material and then write a draft of my section of the book. There would usually be several drafts before a section was finished and for each draft I might refer again to notes or other source materials.

184. Throughout this exercise, I would sometimes mark up copies of Blythe's notes to me, and if I did I would often clear my desk of them when I had finished with them. Because many of the notes Blythe was preparing covered topics about which I was (at first) quite skeptical, I usually looked at Blythe's notes in conjunction with other sources. I was uncomfortable including specific information in the novel unless I could corroborate it in at least a couple of sources. I do not recall precisely how I used the Constantine document, but it is almost certain that I used it in conjunction with other materials.

185. The Constantine document looks to me like a good summary of what I had been reading about Constantine at the time, and the shift from paganism to Christianity.

Chapter 37 -Templars -Priory – Sangreal, and Chapter 58 - lost history, Jesus' marriage and the Grail as bloodline lecture

186. As I have said, Chapter 37 includes material on the Templars, their history, their connection with the Priory, and the word 'sangreal'. Chapter 58 features Langdon and Teabing revealing to Sophie the bloodline theory, as well as some of the imagery in Da Vinci's paintings. Again, these ideas also appeared in the Synopsis, and I re-wrote them for the final version of The Da Vinci Code.

187. I prepared the lecture parts of these chapters in the same general way as I prepared the lecture in chapter 55. A document that I would very likely have looked at while writing such chapters is that entitled "Langdon reveals to Sophie" (D.185 and D.336). Again it was prepared for me by Blythe - she had gotten the material from the sources we were looking at. The first part of the document deals with the history of the Knights Templar and it goes on to give an explanation for what they were looking for under the Temple of Solomon. A lot of this information (including some of the text), I believe, had come from The Hiram Key (D.44), as did some of my research on the Templars. The document then goes on to look at the Priory of Sion, San Graal, and marriage of Jesus and Mary Magdalene; I understand that this information (and some text) appears to have come from Holy Blood, Holy Grail (D.25).

188. This document is an example of one in which Blythe adds a number of notes of her own to tell me to keep in mind points in addition to those which she has set out. The document says "keep in mind these important references" and then there is a list of several points or themes and a corresponding source and page number. Holy Blood, Holy Grail is referenced as well as The Templar Revelation (D.53), Born in Blood (D.55) and The Hiram Key (D.44). For points on the Council of Nicea, Blythe has referenced both Holy Blood, Holy Grail and Templar Revelation. I found Holy Blood, Holy Grail extremely detailed and hard to read, and so I usually went to other books, especially Templar Revelation and The Woman with the Alabaster Jar, to remind myself what they had to say about the subject (by this stage I had already read these books at least once - I still have not read all of Holy Blood, Holy Grail).

189. There is also a note to the effect that the Priory List of Grand Masters can be found on page 131 of Holy Blood, Holy Grai1. At this stage, I had already seen the list many times (for example, Les Dossiers Secrets are available online and I frequently used the internet as a second or third source) and Blythe would have been telling me a convenient way to access it. I do not recall now whether or not I got the list which is primed in The Da Vinci Code from that in Holy Blood, Holy Grail or somewhere else.

190. A further note to me in the document says: "Throughout my readings of all my books, this smell or perfume for some reason keeps: coming up in relation to Mary Magdalene. I have seen this many times." Here she is reminding me that during her research she has seen lots of references to a perfume coming up in connection with the Mary Magdalene. However, I did not work this into my book.

191. The "Constantine" (D.177 and D.322) and "Langdon Reveals to Sophie" (D;185 and D.336) documents are just two of the more than a hundred documents which Blythe prepared for me. I have dealt with them because they contain material from Holy Blood, Holy Grail. Lots of the others she prepared contain material from other books, online sources or other texts. I have described above how I used this type of document and I do not believe my methods of writing are in any way unusual. I will be very surprised if Messrs. Baigent and Leigh did not make copious notes from the sources which they consulted.

192. In chapter 58 of The Da Vinci Code I cite a passage from the Gospel of Philip and another from the Gospel of Mary, which both allude to Mary Magdalene's relationship with Jesus and her important role in his Church. The Gospels of Philip and Mary both come from the Gnostic Gospels and I recall seeing them in many sources. For example, Templar Revelation; The Goddess in the Gospels; and The Gnostic Gospels. Also, one of my research documents "was mm author of 4th gospell_#2849" (D.216 and D.359) includes the passage from the Gospel of Philip.

193. I understand that the same passage from the Gospel of Philip appears in Holy Blood, Holy Grail. I cannot now recall what was my source. I do think that I was aware of the passage from the Gospel of Philip before I looked at Holy Blood, Holy Grail, because the many other sources I looked at which include the Gospel of Philip also include the Gospel of Mary.

194. As I have said, in preparing this statement I have looked back to my research sources, including our books. I see that our copy of Holy Blood, Holy Grail (D.25) is heavily marked up in Blythe's handwriting in a number of places. I am not surprised -we did use the book as a source, after the Synopsis was written and the writing was well underway. But that is not the only reason why the book is marked.

195. As soon as The Da Vinci Code was published and had become a runaway success, I found myself in a firestorm of controversy. I had never experienced this kind of media attention, and it was very difficult at times (especially the criticism from Christians). Often at my book signings, I found myself interrogated publicly by an angry Christian scholar who quizzed me on details of Bible history from the novel. I remember being attacked by one man over my description of the Council of Nicea (specifically the claim that there had been a vote on Jesus' divinity), and I recall feeling defenceless because more than a year had passed since I'd researched and written the novel, and the precise names, dates, places, and facts had faded somewhat in my memory. I quickly realized that if I were going to effectively discuss my work on an international stage, I would need something that Blythe termed "a refresher course".

196. This involved going back to our original resource materials and memorising the details surrounding those ideas about which critics were most upset - the bloodline, the Council of Nicea, Jesus as a husband, etc. Blythe again was on the front lines of gathering information for me. At this time, I know we revisited many of our relevant research materials, including Holy Blood, Holy Grail, and I have little doubt that many of the markings in Holy Blood, Holy Grail (D.25) were made during this "refresher period" after the novel was published. Blythe's help refreshing my memory paid off and after it I was more comfortable dealing with journalists or critics.

197. Also, as I have said, I don't like to write in books, but Blythe writes in books all the time. I know that if she reads a book - that we have bought for research purposes - that has anything to do with any of my novels, she underlines passages as she reads. Blythe is helping me with the research for my new novel, and she is doing just this. So, if she finds a reference to Mary Magdalene, or goddess worship... any of the old subjects, in a new book she still underlines it. She finds this a satisfying thing to do - it reinforces to her that we were on the right track with our earlier research.

198. All of the research books are different pieces of history in theory. Often the books reach the same conclusions - just in a different way. Blythe likes to mark or underline where she finds common links, as it helps her piece the big picture together. Our studies into the origins of the Christian movement and the ancient mysteries continue to this day. Our research and Blythe's note taking is a continual process.

199. Other examples of Blythe marking books in this way are the books Rule by Secrecy, by Jim Marrs (D.50), and The Secret Teachings of All Ages, by Manly P. Hall (D.38). Rule by Secrecy was published in 2000, and The Secret Teachings of All Ages in October 2003. My recollection is that I read Rule by Secrecy in Conway one summer and liked it a lot, but hated the conclusion about aliens, which I thought was somewhat silly. I think this was fairly late during the writing of The Da Vinci Code. The Secret Teachings of All Ages was published too late for me to have made use of it in the writing of The Da Vinci Code.

200. However, my copies of both books are marked in many places, including points which Blythe and I were familiar with by the time we read the books. For example, I see that on page 87 of my copy of Rule by Secrecy (D.50), Blythe has annotated the margin next to the words "Arthurian legend concerning the Holy Grail is closely connected to the controversial notion of a continuing bloodline from Jesus - the Sangreal or royal blood". I can see from one of our documents called "Rosslyn Castle Info" (D.181) that the book appears only to have been looked at by Blythe at the time I was writing the final "Rosslyn" chapters of the book. The fact that Rule by Secrecy (D.50) does not appear in the partial bibliography for the Synopsis supports my recollection. The Secret Teachings of All Ages (D.38) is marked in many places. For example, page 139 is marked despite the fact that the subject matter -the date 25th of December, Constantine and Sol Invictus, is Angels & Demons territory

Names

201. In The Da Vinci Code, in order to amuse myself while writing, and to give added interest to readers, many of my character names are anagrams or are significant in some way.

202. I have played with names in all my books, but I did this a lot in The Da Vinci Code. For example, Jonas Faukman is an anagram of my editor, Jason Kaufman. Silas is a reference to a biblical figure named Silas who was let out of prison by an act of God (The Da Vinci Code, Corgi, page 88). Jerome Collet was inspired by a neighbour of my old pen pal, Sylvie. The Teacher is a reference to Jose Escriva who was the leader of Opus Dei and has often been referred to as "Teacher". Teabing calls himself "The Teacher" to sound more in tune with Opus Dei and thereby trick Silas.

203. Bishop Aringarosa is a play on words; this character looks like a villain, however this a red herring. "Aringa" is herring in Spanish and "Rosa" in Italian is red. Sister Sandrine Bieil was also inspired by a friend of my pen pal Sylvie. Andre Vernet was a French teacher at Exeter. Rene Legaludec was inspired by the Languedoc region in France. Simon Edwards is a dear friend from England. Pamela Gettum is a town librarian in Exeter. Sir Leigh Teabing is, of course, an anagram of the claimants, Messrs. Baigent and Leigh. The character Colbert Sostaque is based on a young boy Colby, to whom I have been a mentor through the Big Brothers Big Sisters program for the last four years. Jean Chaffee is based on my agent's husband. Edouard Delaroches is the archivist at Phillips Exeter Academy. Sauniere, as I explain below, is a playful reference aimed at conspiracy buffs, to the mystery at Rennes-le Chateau, which I did not include in The Da Vinci Code.

Sir Leigh Teabing

204. Sir Leigh Teabing, his house, and even his character did not exist in the early drafts of the book. He is not mentioned in the Synopsis. I initially conceived the character because Langdon and Sophie needed somewhere to rest and eat before moving on to London. As well as providing a safe haven for Sophie and Langdon, I needed to create a character who could say some of the more far-fetched and controversial things that I initially had Langdon saying. I wanted to preserve the integrity of my protagonist. I wanted Langdon to be able to stand back, raise questions and play devil's advocate a little, and also fill in some history. I also did not want Langdon to appear to be too anti Catholic; this is neither the message nor focus of the novel.

205. I included this allusion to Holy Blood, Holy Grail's authors (as opposed to the other three books I cited, see The Da Vinci Code, Corgi, page

339) in the form of the character, Sir Leigh Teabing (an anagram of Baigent & Leigh) for the following reasons:

- Holy Blood, Holy Grail is an older, more traditional book than e Templar Revelation or some of my other sources. It seemed a more fitting match for my Teabing character whom I had crafted as an old British knight.
- I noticed that the letters in "Baigent" were anagram of "Begin at" and that the signature "L Teabing" was an anagram of ' 'Begin at L". That led me to think of a clue which Sophie would decipher -"Begin at L" was to be her clue that L was the first letter of a word and she would go on to decipher that the word she was after was Louvre. As it turned out, I did not use this clue in the book.
- In The Da Vinci Code, Sophie's grandfather called her Princess Sophie, and I thought that calling undue attention to the name "Prince" could be confusing for my readers, so I did not use a Picknett & Prince anagram or reference. I wanted to use the name Starbird, but I thought it sounded too American Indian so decided against it

206. Messrs. Baigent and Leigh are only two of a number of authors who have written about the bloodline story, and yet I went out of my way to mention them for being the ones who brought the theory to mainstream attention. I have been shocked at their reaction: Furthermore I do not really understand it.

207. Over the past ten years, I have placed in my novels the names of more than two dozen close friends and family. The names I choose are always those of people I care for or respect. When I learned that Holy Blood, Holy Grail was the first book to bring the idea of the bloodline into the mainstream, I decided to use the name Leigh Teabing as a playful tribute to Mr. Baigent and Mr. Leigh. I have never once used a novel to denigrate anyone, and most certainly my use of the name Leigh Teabing was no exception, I have seen a document which is entitled "General Statements" and which makes a number of serious allegations against me. The document contains numerous sweeping statements which seem to me to be completely fanciful. It concludes with an assertion that the overall design of Holy Blood,

Holy Grail - the design of its governing themes, its logic, its arguments, has been lifted by me for The Da Vinci Code. This is simply not true.

209. There is a huge amount of information in Holy Blood, Holy Grail that I did not look at in any detail and is simply not in The Da Vinci Code. A comparison of the content of the first half of the two books establishes that. And where there is overlap of ideas, the fact remains that I used Holy Blood, Holy Grail merely as one of a number of reference sources for some of the information which The Da Vinci Code sets out. One of the ideas in Holy Blood, Holy Grail - perhaps even the central idea - is advertised on the back of my copy of the book: "Is it possible Christ did not die on the cross'?". This is not all idea that I would ever have found appealing. Being raised Christian and having attended Bible camp, I am well aware that Christ's crucifixion (and ultimate resurrection) serves as the very core of the Christian faith. It is the promise of life everlasting and that which makes Jesus "the Christ". The resurrection is perhaps the sole controversial Christian topic about which I would not dare write; suggesting a married Jesus is one thing, but undermining the resurrection strikes at the very heart of Christian belief.

210. There is a huge amount of information in The Da Vinci Code that is not in Holy Blood, Ho1y Grail, and I find it absurd to suggest that I have organized and presented my novel in accordance with the same general principles as those in Holy Blood, Holy Grail or that I have plundered not only the facts in Holy Blood, Holy Grail, but also the relationship between the facts, the evidence to support the facts. It is simply not true.

211. As well as mentioning Holy Blood, Holy Grail in The Da Vinci Code, I also mentioned by name three other books I used in my research, namely The Templar Revelation (Picknett & Prince) (D.53); The Woman with the Alabaster Jar (Starbird) (D.59); and The Goddess in the Gospels (Starbird) (D.58) (see The Da Vinci Code, Corgi, page 339). I did this as each of the books I mentioned had played a part in the research I did while writing The Da Vinci Code. I have received a letter of thanks from Margaret Starbird, and Blythe remains in friendly contact with her. Margaret's career has really taken off since publication of The Da Vinci Code. We see her on television specials all the time, and her books are now bestsellers. Lynn Picknett and Clive Prince also sent me a kind letter through their publisher, saying they were very happy with the newfound attention to their books, that they were fans of my work.

212. Henry Lincoln's name does not feature in The Da Vinci Code. There is no particular reason for this. I remember the "Begin at L" reason for using L Teabing and I also remember that Richard Leigh is the name of a friend of mine (he is a famous song writer), but I do not recall anything about Mr Lincoln. I have read an allegation that I made Leigh Teabing a polio victim and a cripple because it was my cruel way of including Mr Lincoln (who apparently walks with a severe limp) in my anagram. This is both untrue and unthinkable to me. I have never met Mr. Lincoln, and I had no idea he had difficulty walking. If I had known, I definitely would have made a different choice. Also, I did not know that Henry Lincoln had made films for the BBC until told this by my English lawyers. I used the BBC in The Da Vinci Code as a device to give Langdon and Teabing a history together. It was also to raise Teabing's status so that Langdon would automatically turn to him for advice. I used the BBC in Angels & Demons as well; the BBC is the only British news agency with which American readers are familiar, and it adds credibility.

Promotion of The Da Vinci Code

213. I am quite sure that a great deal of the success of The Da Vinci Code is down to the excellent promotion the book received. The Da Vinci Code got a huge launch. My first three books were barely promoted. There were more Advance Reader Copies given away for free of The Da Vinci Code than the whole print run for Angels & Demons. I am convinced that The Da Vinci Code would have failed if it had been published by my previous publishers - equally, I think Angels & Demons would have been a big success if published by Random House with as much fanfare as they brought to The Da Vinci Code. Angels & Demons is perhaps even more controversial (it deals with a Pope who had a child), and many people have told me they actually prefer it to The Da Vinci Code.

214. Like The Da Vinci Code, Angels & Demons also touched on some controversial subjects. Angels & Demons is primarily a thriller - a chase, a treasure hunt, and a love story. It's certainly not an anti Catholic book. It's not even a religious book. Much of the novel's action takes place deep inside the arcane world of the Vatican, and some of the factual information revealed there is startling. But I think most people understand that an organization as

old and powerful as the Vatican could not possibly have risen to power without acquiring a few skeletons in its closet. I think the reason Angels & Demons and The Da Vinci Code raised eyebrows is that both books opened some Church closets most people don't even know existed. The final message of both books, though, without a doubt, are positive.

215. It is impossible to ignore the fact that The Da Vinci Code launch was one of the best orchestrated in history. It is still talked about in the industry. Articles have been written specifically on The Da Vinci Code launch (0.362). Steve Rubin and his team should get the credit for the success, (Steve is president of Doubleday, which is, part of Random House, Inc.) He made me meet all the booksellers months before the book came out. Many booksellers were in love with the book when they read the ARC. To release 10,000 ARCs is, I understand, unheard of and this was only on the basis of a first draft. I am sure that the publicity would have had the same effect with Angels & Demons.

216. As part of the launch, Jason and I created a web quest for The Da Vinci Code which is an online treasure hunt to support the book (D.363). This had never been done before in a launch and now all of the big books do it. I must admit, somewhat embarrassingly, that until The Da Vinci Code launch, with the tremendous support booksellers have showed my book, I did not fully understand the role of word of mouth in the process and its power to generate buzz and excitement.

217. The Da Vinci Code is a novel and therefore a work of fiction. While the book's characters and their actions are obviously not real, the artwork, architecture, documents, and secret rituals depicted in this novel all exist (for example, Leonardo da Vinci's paintings, the Gnostic Gospels, Hieros Gamos, etc.) characters and their actions are obviously not real, the artwork, architecture, documents, and select rituals depicted all the novel all exist (for example, Leonardo da Vinci's paintings, the Gnostic Gospels, Hieros Gamos, etc.). These real elements are interpreted and debated by fictional characters. While it is my belief that some of the theories discussed by these characters may have merit, each in individual reader must explore these characters' viewpoints and come to his or her own interpretations. If you read the "FACT" page at the beginning of the novel, you will see it clearly states that the descriptions of artwork, architecture, documents and secret rituals in the novel are accurate. The "FACT" page makes no statement whatsoever about

any of the ancient theories discussed by fictional characters. Interpreting those ideas is left to the reader. My hope in writing this novel was that the story would serve as a catalyst and a springboard for people to discuss the important topics of faith, religion, and history.

218. In closing, I would like to restate that I remain astounded by the Claimants' choice to file this plagiarism suit. For them to suggest, as I understand they do, that I have "hijacked and exploited" their work is simply untrue.

Statement of Truth

I believe that the facts stated in this Witness Statement are true.

Full name: DAN BROWN

Position Author

Date 21 December 2005

Information Launchpad

The Information Launchpad provides tips and tricks on how to use the Internet to discover interesting information about books by Dan Brown.

Google Web

Start with a search on "Dan Brown" – be sure to include the quotes.

http://www.google.com/search?hl=en&lr=&c2coff=1&tab=nw&ie=UTF-8&q=%22dan+brown%22&sa=N&wxob=0

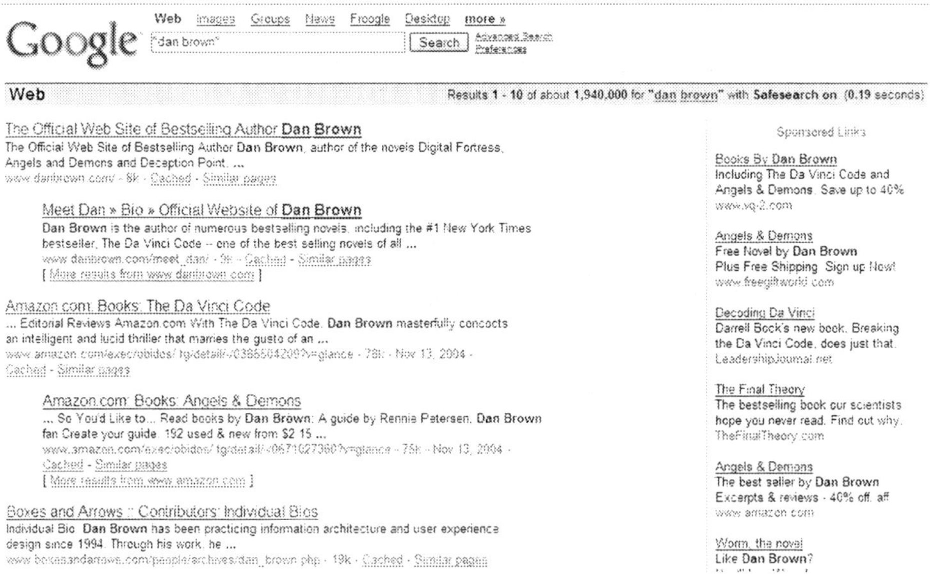
Google
Web Images Groups News Froogle Desktop more »
"dan brown"
Search
Web
Results 1 - 10 of about 1,940,000 for "dan brown" with Safesearch on (0.19 seconds)
The Official Web Site of Bestselling Author Dan Brown
The Official Web Site of Bestselling Author Dan Brown, author of the novels Digital Fortress, Angels and Demons and Deception Point. ...
Meet Dan » Bio » Official Website of Dan Brown
Dan Brown is the author of numerous bestselling novels, including the #1 New York Times bestseller, The Da Vinci Code -- one of the best selling novels of all ...
Amazon.com: Books: The Da Vinci Code
... Editorial Reviews Amazon.com With The Da Vinci Code, Dan Brown masterfully concocts an intelligent and lucid thriller that marries the gusto of an ...
Amazon.com: Books: Angels & Demons
... So You'd Like to... Read books by Dan Brown: A guide by Rennie Petersen, Dan Brown fan Create your guide. 192 used & new from $2.15 ...
Boxes and Arrows :: Contributors: Individual Bios
Individual Bio Dan Brown has been practicing information architecture and user experience design since 1994. Through his work, he ...
Sponsored Links
Books By Dan Brown
Including The Da Vinci Code and Angels & Demons. Save up to 40%
Angels & Demons
Free Novel by Dan Brown
Plus Free Shipping. Sign up Now!
Decoding Da Vinci
Darrell Bock's new book, Breaking the Da Vinci Code, does just that.
The Final Theory
The bestselling book our scientists hope you never read. Find out why.
Angels & Demons
The best seller by Dan Brown
Excerpts & reviews - 40% off. aff
Worm, the novel
Like Dan Brown?

"The Official Web Site of Bestselling Author Dan Brown" is, as you might expect, a good place to start.

Google Images

A Google Images search on "Da Vinci Code" brings up a lot of identical pictures of the book's cover.

http://images.google.com/images?q=%22da+vinci+code%22&hl=en&btnG =Google+Search

More interesting: add a country suffix using the Google "site" operator, as in "Da Vinci Code" site:.uk.

http://images.google.com/images?hl=en&lr=&safe=active&c2coff=1&q=% 22da+vinci+code%22+site%3A.uk&btnG=Search

This brings up Rosslyn Chapel as #1, followed by images of the UK cover, which has a very different color scheme from the US version.

Google News & Alerts

A Google News search on the following URL will bring up the latest news on the quoted phrase "Da Vinci Code."

http://news.google.com/news?q=%22da%20vinci%20code%22&hl=en&lr= &c2coff=1&safe=active&sa=N&tab=wn

At the bottom of the answer set, click on the link that reads "Get the latest news on da-vinci-code."

New! Get the latest news on **da-vinci-code** with Google News Alerts.

Gooooooooooogle ▶

Result Page: 1 2 3 4 5 6 7 8 9 10 **Next**

You will be presented with the opportunity to set up a Google Alert.

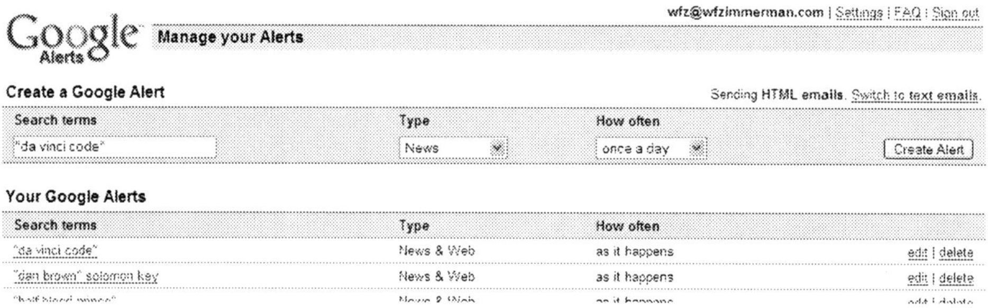
wfz@wfzimmerman.com | Settings | FAQ | Sign out
Google Alerts
Manage your Alerts
Create a Google Alert
Sending HTML emails. Switch to text emails.
Search terms
Type
How often
"da vinci code"
News
once a day
Create Alert
Your Google Alerts
Search terms
Type
How often
"da vinci code"
News & Web
as it happens
edit | delete
"dan brown" solomon key
News & Web
as it happens
edit | delete

Select type "News & Web" and "as it happens" (if you bought this book, you want to know *immediately* ...)

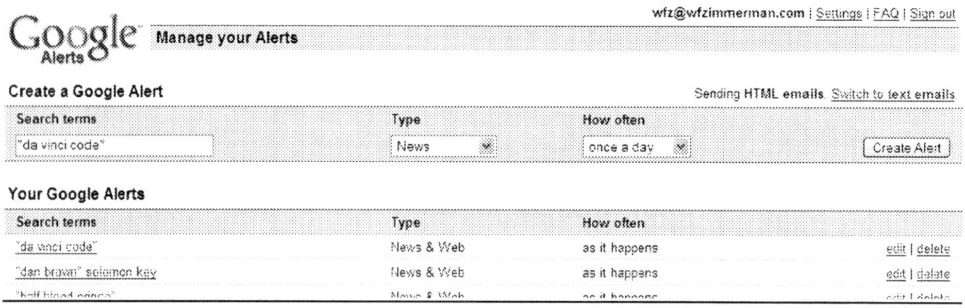
wfz@wfzimmerman.com | Settings | FAQ | Sign out
Google Alerts
Manage your Alerts
Create a Google Alert
Sending HTML emails. Switch to text emails
Search terms
Type
How often
"da vinci code"
News
once a day
Create Alert
Your Google Alerts
Search terms
Type
How often
"da vinci code"
News & Web
as it happens
edit | delete
"dan brown" solomon key
News & Web
as it happens
edit | delete

Set up a Google Alert.

Google Video

Google's new Video feature enables you to search for TV programs where Dan Brown or his works are discussed. Here are a few sample links:

"Da Vinci Code"	http://video.google.com/videosearch?q=%22da+vinci+code%22&btnG=Google+Search
The Solomon Key"	http://video.google.com/videosearch?q=%22the+solomon+key%22
"Dan Brown"	http://video.google.com/videosearch?q=%22dan+brown%22

The results look like this.

Google Video BETA
"da vinci code"
Search Video
Preferences
Video
Results 1 - 9 of about 9 for "da vinci code" (0.03 secon
Jeopardy!
... up with the correct response. So the wagering will be very important. Let's go to the middle first to you, Jonathan. You came up with "the da Vinci code." You are right, and your Wager... Almost everything. $5,999. Taking you up to $11,999 as we go to Steve Kaplan. Do we find "the da Vinci code"?...
ABC - ABC Network - Thu Jan 20 2005 at 7:00 PM PST - 30 minutes
CBS 5 Eyewitness News at 11
... stages. >> Investigators say they know who the growers are, but they have made no arrests yet. >>> Even before the best-selling novel, "the da Vinci code," Art lovers were intrigued by the mysteries in the florentine master, especially the Mona Lisa and The enigmatic smile. One of the secret mace...
CBS - CBS Network - Sat Jan 22 2005 at 1:37 AM PST - 35 minutes
CBS 5 Eyewitness News at 11
... stages. >> Investigators say they know who the growers are, but they have made no arrests yet. >>> Even before the best-selling novel, "the da Vinci code," Art lovers were intrigued by the mysteries in the florentine master, especially the Mona Lisa and The enigmatic smile. One of the secret mace...
CBS - CBS Network - Fri Jan 21 2005 at 11:00 PM PST - 35 minutes
Early Today
Business/financial news.
... Is connected, efficient, beautiful. Detailed case studies at Sprint Com. >>> A discovery in Florence, Italy, is like something out of the da Vinci code. Researchers discovered a

A great way of finding relevant video "ex post facto", but of course, there is one huge drawback, which is that this is not a "TV Guide" feature that alerts you to upcoming transmissions of interest.

Google Desktop

Make sure you're getting the most out of your own resources by downloading Google Desktop at http://desktop.google.com/. You can use this clean and extremely fast tool to find those interesting e-mails, web pages, and documents that you read a while ago but have now misplaced. At the current cost ($0), a must-have for anyone who likes to gather secrets, mysteries, and arcana–then find them again. "Information overload" may be the greatest camouflage ever invented for of the world's secret societies!

By way of illustration, one search early in this project turned up 34 e-mails and 11 documents, including both a Word document and an Excel spreadsheet.

Web Images Groups News Froogle Desktop more »
"da vinci code"
Search Desktop
Desktop: All - 34 emails - 11 files - 0 chats - 0 web history
Unauthorized Dan Brown Update.doc
Da Vinci Code. Now every time someone writes about "The Da Vinci Code .. The Da Vinci Code
Book title Author(s) Fred's comments The Da Vinci Code
My Documents\Nimble Boo...\Unauthorized Dan Brown Update.doc - 16 cached - 12:45pm
hpb_marketing (version latest).xls
38349.00 9.94 1.00 0.35 6.46 2.30 0.00 0.00 4.16 310 (dan brown) 290 (da vinci) 120 (da vinci code) 160 .. vinci) 120 (da vinci code) 160 (solomon
My Documents\Nimble Book...\hpb_marketing (version latest).xls - 4 cached - 9:34am
[2004/11/24] "Da Vinci Code" : 385,000 pages (+1.32%)
Da Vinci Code" returned 385,000 pages, a +1.32% change since yesterday. Related: http:services .newsgator.com/subscriber/Related.aspx?relurl=http%3a%2f%2fg-metrics.com
g-metrics custom feed - 4:11am

Google Desktop uncovers the long-lost secrets of my hard drive.

G-metrics

The G-metrics web site will let you track the "Google Count" of a word or Google search phrase. For example, here is the Google Count for the search phrase "Da Vinci Code" (http://www.g-metrics.com/index.php?act=details&ID=2920)

google query: "Da Vinci Code"

Title: "Da Vinci Code" [add to my list]
Lang. restriction: none

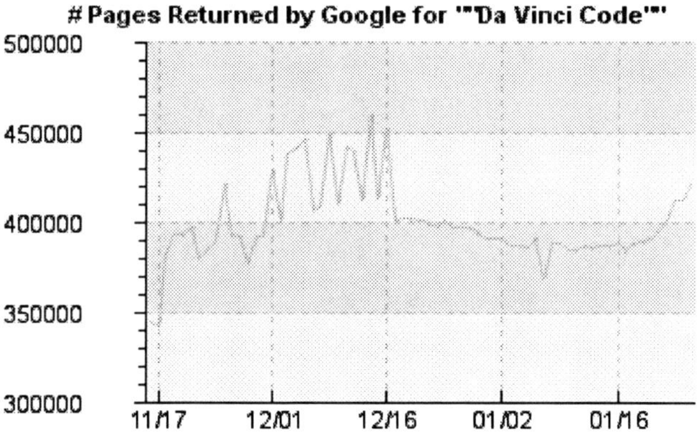

Pages Returned by Google for '"Da Vinci Code"'
500000
450000
400000
350000
300000
11/17
12/01
12/16
01/02
01/16

meta

- The URI to TrackBack this page is: http://g-metrics.com/trackback/2920
- tab delimeted format
- RSS Feed

7-day results

Date	Googlecount	Change (%)
2005/01/26	421,000	+2.18%
2005/01/25	412,000	+0.00%

Hip to RSS? Add this feed:http://g-metrics.com/rss.php?k=2920 XML

RSS Feeds

RSS feeds are a popular way of downloading frequently updated content like news stories. You use a news feed reader to "subscribe" to a web address (http://...) that is an XML document (ending in .xml). News feed readers come in all varieties, from standalone software to tools built into e-mail or browsers. The common theme is that when you see a little icon saying "RSS" or "XML", you click (or do something else that's simple) to add the RSS feed to your list of "subscriptions." If you're interested in learning more, check out my website,

http://www.wfzimmerman.com/index.php?topic=RSSetc

If you're already hip to RSS, here is a list of RSS feeds that you may find of interest.

OPML file

The Outline Markup Processing Language (OPML) is, for historical reasons, the standard means for transferring a list of RSS, RDF, or Atom news feeds from one place to another. Most feed readers can import OPML files–look for a command like "Import OPML" or "Import list of feeds." I have created a special OPML file that includes information for a variety of RSS feeds relating to Dan Brown and his books. You can download it at http://www.wfzimmerman.com > My Downloads.

Amazon.com Books

To find books containing the words "Da Vinci Code" in the title but with author *not* Dan Brown, go to Amazon.com > Books > Search > Advanced Search (http://www.amazon.com/exec/obidos/ats-query-page/). Scroll down to "Power Search." Enter the search syntax "title: da vinci code and not author: dan brown".

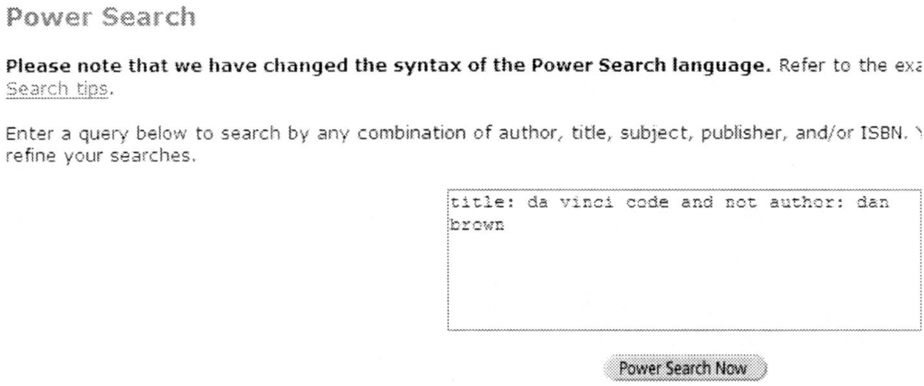
Power Search
Please note that we have changed the syntax of the Power Search language. Refer to the exa
Search tips.
Enter a query below to search by any combination of author, title, subject, publisher, and/or ISBN.
refine your searches.
title: da vinci code and not author: dan brown
Power Search Now

IMDB

The Internet Movie Data Base, operated by Amazon.com, is a fundamental source.

The movie home page http://www.imdb.com/title/tt0382625/ and includes links to pages for each of the key personnel in the movie.

Producer: Brian Grazer.	IMDB producer credits: http://www.imdb.com/name/nm0004976/
Director: Ron Howard.	IMDB director credits: http://www.imdb.com/name/nm0000165/
Screenwriter(s): Akiva Goldsman.	IMDB screenwriter credits http://www.imdb.com/name/nm0326040/
Cinematographer: Salvatore Totino	IMDB Pro cinematographer credits: http://www.imdb.com/name/nm0869379/
Composer: James Horner	IMDB composer credits http://www.imdb.com/name/nm0000035/
Tom Hanks	http://www.imdb.com/name/nm0000158/
Audrey Tautou	http://www.imdb.com/name/nm0851582/
Jean Reno	http://www.imdb.com/name/nm0000606/?

IMDB message boards:
http://www.imdb.com/title/tt0382625/board/threads/

E-Bay Products

Buy collectible first editions of "Da Vinci Code" on eBay by going to http://www.ebay.com > Buy (http://hub.ebay.com/buy?ssPageName=h:h:cat:US) Select

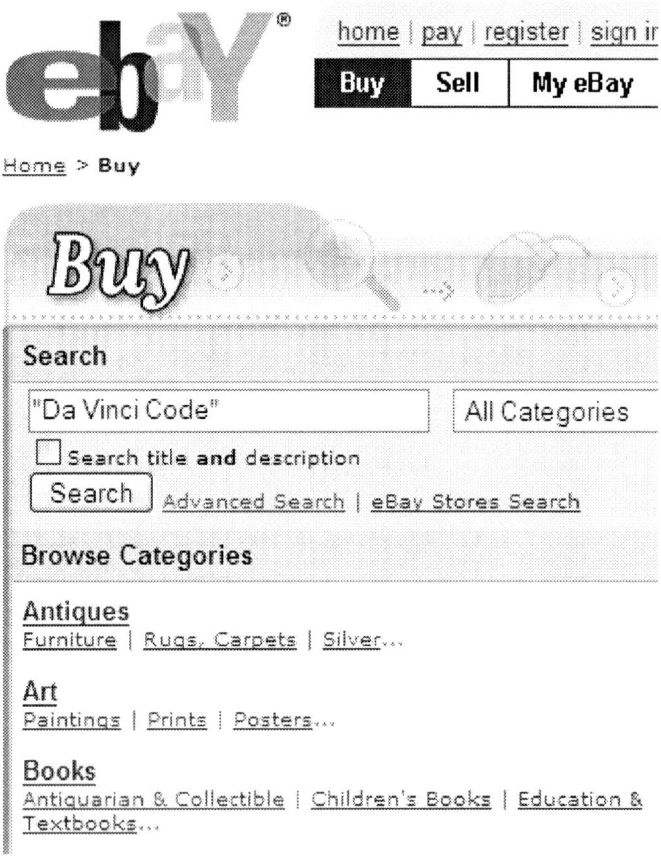
home | pay | register | sign in
Buy
Sell
My eBay
Home > Buy
Buy
Search
"Da Vinci Code"
All Categories
Search title and description
Search
Advanced Search | eBay Stores Search
Browse Categories
Antiques
Furniture | Rugs, Carpets | Silver...
Art
Paintings | Prints | Posters...
Books
Antiquarian & Collectible | Children's Books | Education & Textbooks...

A snapshot of a few sample results is shown here.

10 items found for "Da Vinci Code" in Antiquarian & Collectible
Add to Favorites
List View | Picture Gallery
Sort by: Time: newly listed
Customize Display
Compare
Item Title
PayPal
Price
Bids
Time Listed
Dan Brown Da Vinci Code 1st Ed 1st Print Fine/Fine DJ
$100.00
Nov-17 15:53
The Da Vinci Code by Dan Brown (2003)
$6.99
Nov-15 07:10
True 1st/1st JOHN GRISHAM ~ TESTAMENT *Da Vinci Code x2
$4.95
$14.95 Buy It Now
Nov-14 19:55
The DA VINCI CODE - Dan Brown - ARC Proof -ADVANCE COPY
$15.00
2
Nov-14 19:30
Dan Brown~THE DA VINCI CODE~Signed 1st printing
Booksense Book of the Year winner~Publishing phenomenon
$395.00
$420.00 Buy It Now
Nov-14 15:48

Track the sales of collectible books by Dan Brown using this RSS feed:

http://www.freebiddingtools.com/rss/feeds/9224 XML

Technorati

With a Technorati ID & password, you can create a Watch List for any book or product at Amazon.com that has an ISBN or ASIN (an Amazon.com code).

"The Da Vinci Code" is usually visible in the Top 100 books at http://www.technorati.com/live/products.html, and if you click on the little "chat" icon

You will be taken to a page that looks like this.

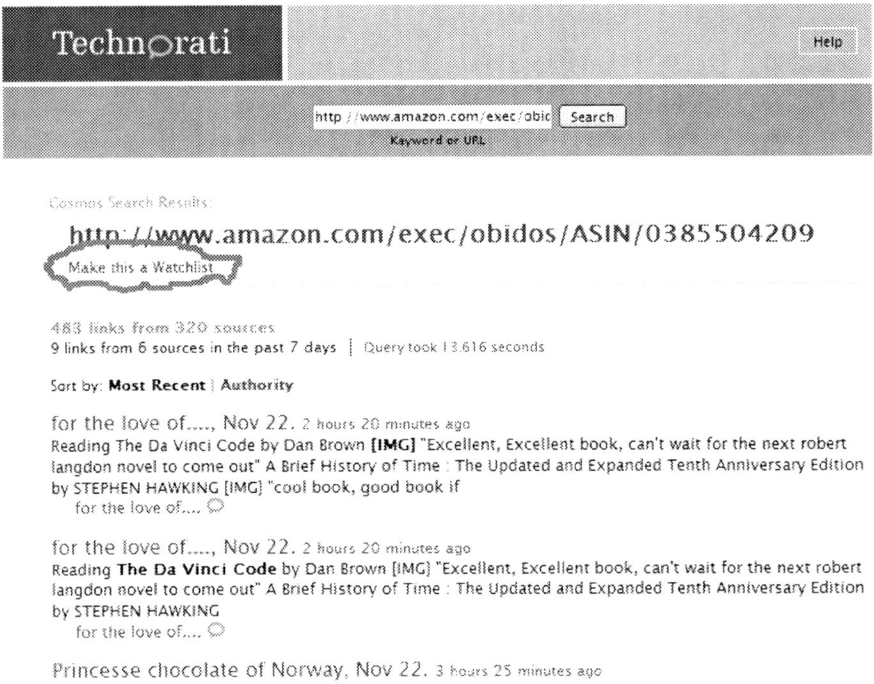
Technorati
Help
http://www.amazon.com/exec/obic
Search
Keyword or URL
Cosmos Search Results:
http://www.amazon.com/exec/obidos/ASIN/0385504209
Make this a Watchlist
483 links from 320 sources
9 links from 6 sources in the past 7 days | Query took 13.616 seconds
Sort by: Most Recent | Authority
for the love of...., Nov 22. 2 hours 20 minutes ago
Reading The Da Vinci Code by Dan Brown [IMG] "Excellent, Excellent book, can't wait for the next robert langdon novel to come out" A Brief History of Time : The Updated and Expanded Tenth Anniversary Edition by STEPHEN HAWKING [IMG] "cool book, good book if
for the love of....
for the love of...., Nov 22. 2 hours 20 minutes ago
Reading The Da Vinci Code by Dan Brown [IMG] "Excellent, Excellent book, can't wait for the next robert langdon novel to come out" A Brief History of Time : The Updated and Expanded Tenth Anniversary Edition by STEPHEN HAWKING
for the love of....
Princesse chocolate of Norway, Nov 22. 3 hours 25 minutes ago

Click on "Make this a Watchlist." Technorati finds every time that a blog links to the Amazon version of "Da Vinci Code."

Now every time someone writes about "The Da Vinci Code" in a blog, your RSS reader will pull the results to you. Here's what one snapshot of recent discussions looks like rendered in NewsGator, a Outlook-based reader.

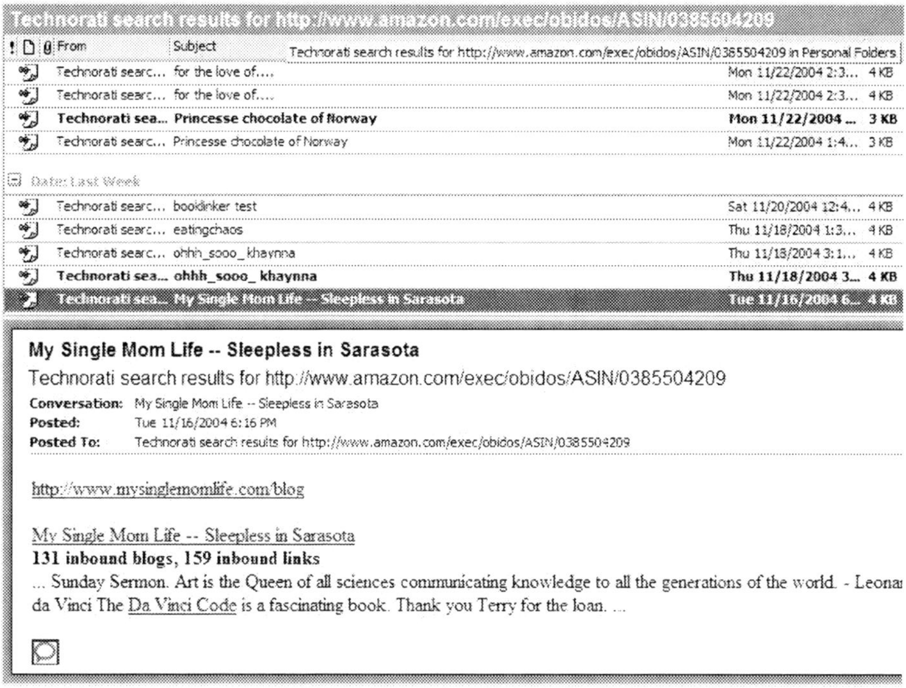
Technorati search results for http://www.amazon.com/exec/obidos/ASIN/0385504209
From
Subject
Technorati search results for http://www.amazon.com/exec/obidos/ASIN/0385504209 in Personal Folders
Technorati searc... for the love of.... Mon 11/22/2004 2:3... 4 KB
Technorati searc... for the love of.... Mon 11/22/2004 2:3... 4 KB
Technorati sea... Princesse chocolate of Norway Mon 11/22/2004 ... 3 KB
Technorati searc... Princesse chocolate of Norway Mon 11/22/2004 1:4... 3 KB
Date: Last Week
Technorati searc... bookdinker test Sat 11/20/2004 12:4... 4 KB
Technorati searc... eatingchaos Thu 11/18/2004 1:3... 4 KB
Technorati searc... ohhh_sooo_khaynna Thu 11/18/2004 3:1... 4 KB
Technorati sea... ohhh_sooo_ khaynna Thu 11/18/2004 3... 4 KB
Technorati sea... My Single Mom Life -- Sleepless in Sarasota Tue 11/16/2004 6... 4 KB
My Single Mom Life -- Sleepless in Sarasota
Technorati search results for http://www.amazon.com/exec/obidos/ASIN/0385504209
Conversation: My Single Mom Life -- Sleepless in Sarasota
Posted: Tue 11/16/2004 6:16 PM
Posted To: Technorati search results for http://www.amazon.com/exec/obidos/ASIN/0385504209
http://www.mysinglemomlife.com/blog
My Single Mom Life -- Sleepless in Sarasota
131 inbound blogs, 159 inbound links
... Sunday Sermon. Art is the Queen of all sciences communicating knowledge to all the generations of the world. - Leonar
da Vinci The Da Vinci Code is a fascinating book. Thank you Terry for the loan. ...

Usenet

Usenet is the "mother of all Internet discussion groups" – the world's oldest collection of topical newsgroups. There do not appear to be any Usenet groups specifically devoted to Dan Brown or "The Da Vinci Code," so you will have to do a little bit of digging to find your way to the many interesting discussions that are, as they say in the X-Files, "out there."

If you are using Outlook Express or another NNTP news reader (stick with Outlook Express if that doesn't mean anything to you), the best strategy is to find a topical newsgroup where you like the general tone of discussions, then raise the subject of Dan Brown and "Da Vinci Code" there. For example, I found some great discussions in one of my favorite newsgroups, news:rec.arts.sf.written.

The other main approach that you can take is to search across all of Usenet via Google Groups (http://groups.google.com). A Google Groups search on "Da Vinci Code" produces results like this:

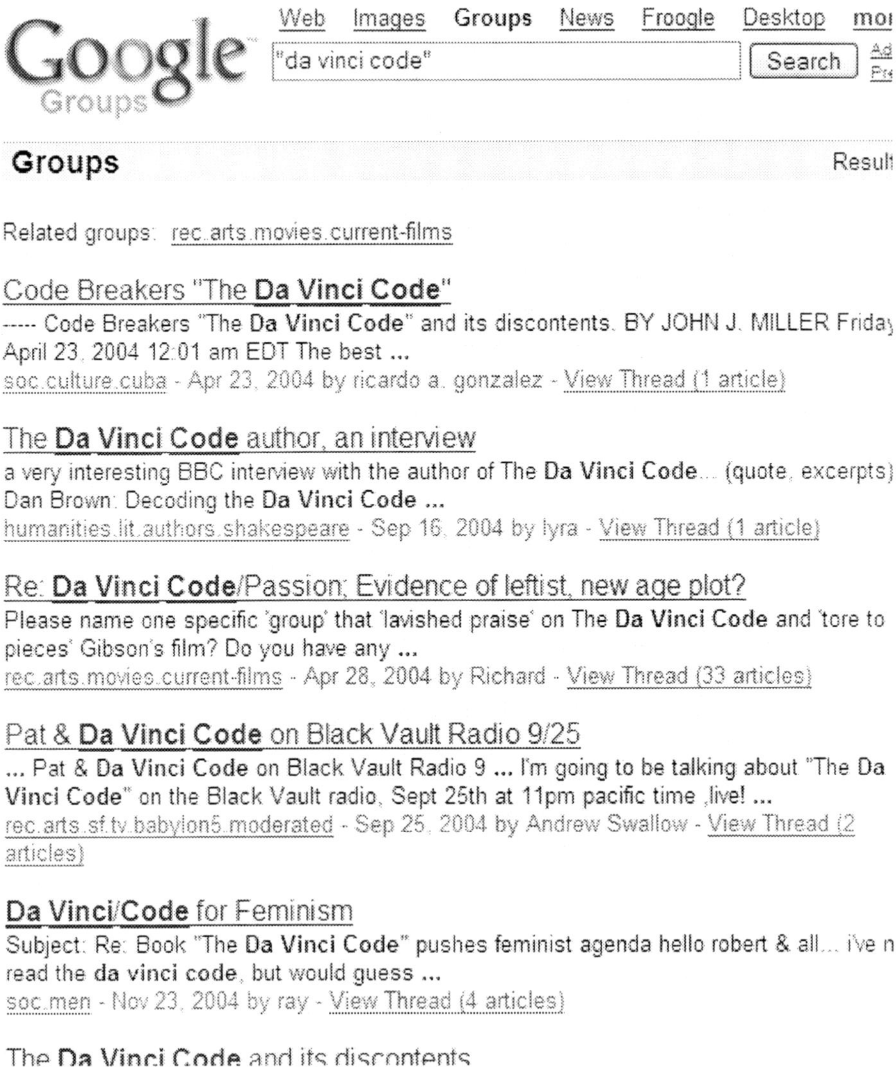
Web Images Groups News Froogle Desktop
"da vinci code"
Search
Google Groups
Groups
Related groups: rec.arts.movies.current-films
Code Breakers "The Da Vinci Code"
----- Code Breakers "The Da Vinci Code" and its discontents. BY JOHN J. MILLER
April 23, 2004 12:01 am EDT The best ...
soc.culture.cuba - Apr 23, 2004 by ricardo a. gonzalez - View Thread (1 article)
The Da Vinci Code author, an interview
a very interesting BBC interview with the author of The Da Vinci Code... (quote, excerpts)
Dan Brown: Decoding the Da Vinci Code ...
humanities.lit.authors.shakespeare - Sep 16, 2004 by lyra - View Thread (1 article)
Re: Da Vinci Code/Passion: Evidence of leftist, new age plot?
Please name one specific 'group' that 'lavished praise' on The Da Vinci Code and 'tore to pieces' Gibson's film? Do you have any ...
rec.arts.movies.current-films - Apr 28, 2004 by Richard - View Thread (33 articles)
Pat & Da Vinci Code on Black Vault Radio 9/25
... Pat & Da Vinci Code on Black Vault Radio 9 ... I'm going to be talking about "The Da Vinci Code" on the Black Vault radio, Sept 25th at 11pm pacific time ,live! ...
rec.arts.sf.tv.babylon5.moderated - Sep 25, 2004 by Andrew Swallow - View Thread (2 articles)
Da Vinci/Code for Feminism
Subject: Re: Book "The Da Vinci Code" pushes feminist agenda hello robert & all...
read the da vinci code, but would guess ...
soc.men - Nov 23, 2004 by ray - View Thread (4 articles)
The Da Vinci Code and its discontents

Google Groups (Usenet) search on "The Da Vinci Code."

You'll notice that this Google Groups search uncovers quite a hodge-podge of discussions in places ranging from soc.culture.cuba to rec.arts.sf.tv.babylon5.moderated. That's a fair reflection of reality. There is a great wealth of material available in Usenet, but it is loosely organized and mostly uncensored. The best strategies that I have found for unearthing useful information related to Dan Brown and "The Da Vinci Code" in Google Groups are as follows:

- Use highly specific keyword searches including the Google "+" mandatory operator. `"Da Vinci Code" +Teabing` will take you straight to discussions that mention that character.
- Click on the threads that have the highest number of articles, then read the stuff at the beginning of the thread (before it went off-topic or people began to repeat themselves).

Mailing Lists

In my experience, the best place to find mailing lists for discussion of "The Da Vinci Code" is Yahoo! Groups (http://www.yahoogroups.com). No only does Yahoo! Groups have more lists than other sites, but–because of its high volume–it also has more highly evolved anti-spam features.

A search on the quoted string "Da Vinci Code" turned up 23 lists whose title or summary included the phrase "Da Vinci Code." I signed up for the four groups that are specifically about "Da Vinci Code" as a book and that have more than 150 members.

There are several other large groups that are more in the nature of religious groups discussing Gnostic themes that also happen to discuss "Da Vinci Code." Those groups may be worthwhile if your interest is more in terms of a spiritual quest than in terms of reading best-selling novels.

One other place that is worth considering is the Google Groups Beta service at http://groups-beta.google.com. The great thing about this is that it combines Usenet and mailing lists in a single clean Googlesque interface. The negative is that there aren't many mailing lists so far. On the other hand, that makes this a great place to set up your very own "Da Vinci Code" discussion list … when Google moves the Groups Beta to production, the volume will go up, and you'll be in a good position to get all the new mailing list members!

Colophon

This book was produced using Microsoft Word and Adobe Acrobat.

Heading fonts and the body text inside the book are in Palatino Linotype, chosen because it is a nimble-looking font. Quotations are in Courier New. Heading fonts are rendered in gold (RGB 170, 141, 75) the predominant type color on the cover of "The Da Vinci Code.

The American Heritage® Dictionary of the English Language, Fourth Edition, copyright © 2000 by Houghton Mifflin Company defines col·o·phon as follows:

> An ancient Greek city of Asia Minor northwest of Ephesus. It was famous for its cavalry.

Along the same lines, Webster's Revised Unabridged, copyright 1996, 1998, MICRA, Inc.:

> \Col"o*phon\ (k[o^]l"[-o]*f[o^]n), n. [L. colophon finishing stroke, Gr. kolofw`n; cf. L. culmen top, collis hill. Cf. Holm.] An inscription, monogram, or cipher, containing the place and date of publication, printer's name, etc., formerly placed on the last page of a book.

I always look for an appropriate and substantive "finishing stroke" to finish each book. In this case, what could be more appropriate than this ambigram, created using Ambigram.Matic's Ambigram Generator?[41]

[41] http://ambigram.matic.com/ambigram.htm

Breinigsville, PA USA
11 April 2010
235903BV00001B/131/A

9 780975 447994